"You said that no pressure and no price would persuade you to share my bed."

Sholto continued silkily. "I'm calling your bluff. If you move into my house and live with me, I will settle your brother's debts."

For a count of ten paralyzed seconds, Molly gaped at him with startled green eyes and parted lips. "You're not serious," she said when she could finally unpeel her tongue from the roof of her mouth.

"I want you…and you want your brother off the hook. A fair exchange or an abuse of power?" Sholto mused with galling cool. "I shall leave you to decide which."

LYNNE GRAHAM was born in Northern Ireland and has been a keen romance reader since her teens. She is very happily married, with an understanding husband who has learned to cook since she started to write. Her three children keep her on her toes. She also has a very large Old English sheepdog, who knocks everything over, and two cats. When time allows, Lynne is a keen gardener.

Books by Lynne Graham

LYNNE GRAHAM

Mistress and Mother

Harlequin Books

TORONTO • NEW YORK • LONDON
AMSTERDAM • PARIS • SYDNEY • HAMBURG
STOCKHOLM • ATHENS • TOKYO • MILAN
MADRID • WARSAW • BUDAPEST • AUCKLAND

For my daughter, Rachel, whose love and advice
are always welcome.

ISBN 0-373-11937-2

MISTRESS AND MOTHER

First North American Publication 1998.

Copyright © 1997 by Lynne Graham.

CHAPTER ONE

As THE snow became a blinding white blur, the wipers struggled to keep a wedge of the car windscreen clear. Then, finally, the narrow, twisting road began to climb. Not much further now. Molly cut down another gear, praying that the tyres would keep a grip on the treacherously slippery gradient.

That petrol-pump attendant had warned her that it would be crazy to attempt the lake road in snow but Molly often flew in the face of sound advice. And her stubborn determination to reach Freddy's isolated home had its deepest roots in guilt. She hadn't gone to his funeral. Her fiancé, Donald, had offered to go with her as moral support but she still hadn't been able to face such an ordeal.

The small car slid slowly back down the hill again. Molly gritted her teeth and started up it again. She was almost there. The house sat at the top of the hill overlooking the lake. Over four years had passed, but she still remembered that misty view of the moorland running down to the water's edge. Her face stiffened and shadowed, fingers clenching round the wheel. She also remembered the slavish way she had tried to follow Sholto out of the room when a call had come for him. Freddy had caught her back, his wise old eyes almost pitying as he scanned her anxious, adoring face.

'Don't cling, my dear. It'll put wings on his feet. You can't tame a wild bird and keep it in a cage... Sholto isn't a domesticated animal. This is all new to him. Hasten slowly.'

But she hadn't listened, she conceded sickly, hadn't seen, hadn't been able to focus on anything but her own desperate need to be as close to Sholto as his skin. And the more he had stepped back from her, the harder she had pushed, not even knowing then, not even suspecting that Sholto's heart could never, ever be hers. She wore another man's ring now but remembrance still cramped her stomach and her tired legs trembled, the foot she had on the accelerator pressing down with sudden involuntary force.

She cried out in fright as the car slewed violently sideways and then skidded with unnatural, terrifying grace off the road. Her heartbeat thundered in her eardrums as she brought the hatchback to a shuddering halt, headlights gleaming out over the daunting expanse of dark water only yards away. Swallowing hard, she tried to reverse back up onto the road but the tyres spun on the boggy, snow-slick ground and the car stayed where it was.

Finally, she detached her seatbelt and climbed out into the teeth of the wind. She would *walk* up the hill. Dear heaven, she might have killed herself! The car might have kept right on going and the lake was deep.

Grabbing up her shoulder bag, shivering convulsively as the wind blew snow into her face and snatched up her long fall of russet hair to whip it across her eyes and mouth, she pulled up the hood of her light jacket and locked the car. It was well after eight. Freddy's housekeeper wasn't even expecting her and now Molly would have to ask her for a bed for the night into the bargain.

Stupid, *stupid*, Molly castigated herself as she toiled up the hill. Why avoid the funeral and then drive all the way to the Lake District just to collect the old vase which Freddy had left her and leave a few flowers at the cemetery? Her brother, Nigel, had been stunned when he'd realised she could have gone to the funeral and the scene which had followed that revelation had left Molly feeling sick with irrational guilt.

'The perfect opportunity...and you didn't take it?' Nigel had condemned in disbelief. 'But Sholto would've been there! You could've talked to him then.'

'Don't, Nigel...' his wife, Lena, had begged, her strained eyes swimming with tears. 'This isn't Molly's problem. It's ours.'

'Will you still feel like that when you and the kids have no roof over your heads?' Nigel had demanded, the stress of recent months etched in his thin, boyish features. 'What would it cost Molly to go and eat a bit of humble pie? *I'd* do it...but I can't get near him!'

Now the snow was falling thicker and heavier, crunching over the sides of her shoes and freezing her feet. In no mood to dwell on her brother's desperate financial problems, Molly dug icy hands into her pockets and plodded on up the hill. The dark, unadorned bulk of the house loomed just where the road dropped down again and she felt quite weak with relief. There were no lights visible but on a bad night like this an elderly woman might already be tucked up warm in her bed.

The freezing wind slashing with cruel efficiency through her inadequate clothing, Molly rushed to press the old-fashioned doorbell. A couple of endless minutes later, she hit it again, and then more quickly the third and the fourth time, dismay powering her as she stood back and peered up at the black, unrevealing windows in search of an encouraging chink of light.

She had assumed that the housekeeper would be here for at least another week. But maybe she *didn't* live in. As that possibility occurred to Molly for the very first time, she could've kicked herself for blithely assuming that Freddy's housekeeper lived on the premises. If the house was empty, she was in deep trouble. She might freeze to death spending the night in the car. She didn't even have a travel rug to wrap around herself. When she had left home after lunch it had been a beautiful sunny day and she hadn't paid the slightest heed to the weather forecast.

Panic firing her, Molly trudged round to the back of the house. Obviously there was nobody inside. She peered at the snow-covered ground, prowling up and down until she found a suitable stone. Fingers almost numb, she yanked off her jacket and wound it round her arm, her hand fiercely gripping the stone as she braced herself in front of the small window beside the back door. Taking a deep breath, she swung her arm up full force and smashed the pane. Stepping back, she breathed out in a rush, shook herself free of broken glass and dragged on her jacket again.

Reaching inside with great care, she undid the latch and the frame swung out. Planting her chilled hands on the stone sill, she hauled herself up with a groan of effort and crawled on her knees through the open window, slowly feeling her way onto the kitchen worktop. A startled yelp of pain escaped her as a splinter of glass pierced her knee. But even as she stilled in exasperated acknowledgement of her own foolishness she had the terrifying sense of something big moving fast towards her in the darkness.

As a pair of powerful hands snatched her up into mid-air, she screamed so hard she hurt her throat. Then she was hitting the stone floor face down, all the breath driven from her body by the impact, hands flailing in wild terror as a suffocating weight dug into her spine. Hard, imprisoning fingers raked down her arms to entrap her frantic hands and then as quickly loosened their grip and freed her again.

A burst of Italian invective assailed her ears at the same time as the knee braced on her back was removed and the fluorescent light above flickered on. Quivering with stark terror, Molly jerked up and rolled back against the cupboards like a cornered animal bracing itself for another attack. When her glazed eyes focused on the male standing over her, she simply stared, wide-eyed with disbelief.

'*Madre di Dio*...I could have broken every bone in your body!' Sholto raked down at her in driving condemnation.

So deep in shock, she was incapable of response, Molly's huge green eyes clung to the six-foot-three male towering over her as if he were a terrifying apparition, her cheekbones prominent with stress, her complexion bone-white, her lips bloodlessly compressed.

With a stifled imprecation, Sholto dropped down into an athletic crouch and ran lean brown hands gently down over her limp arms and thighs. His startlingly handsome features clenched as he saw the blood seeping messily through the torn knee of her black tights. He completed his check for any further injury before he drew back.

Molly still couldn't move. Slowly, she closed her eyes, meaning to open them again and see if he was still there but the impersonal touch of his beautifully shaped hands still lingered like the kiss of fire on her frozen flesh, blocking out all rational thought. Four years since she had seen him, not since that fateful night he had walked out on her to go to his cousin, Pandora. Her paralysis gave and she started to shake uncontrollably, the aftermath of choking fear and horror at his appearance combining to threaten a tidal wave of emotion.

'What the hell were you playing at?' Sholto bent down and scooped her up into his arms as if she weighed no more than a feather. 'And what are you doing here at this hour of the night?'

Her teeth bit down on her tongue, releasing the sickly sweet tang of blood into her dry mouth. The pain helped, controlling the great lump blossoming in her throat, the acrid stinging at the back of her eyes. But it was nothing to the pain she remembered. That had been pain like a poisoned knife, slipping in on a cruel, teeth-clenching thrust and then teaching her that there was yet worse to come and that the human mind could suffer as much agony as the human body.

He was settling her down on a hard chair and abstractedly she recalled Freddy's eccentric loathing of any form of soft comfort or cosiness. No central heating, wide-open windows even in winter, no clutter and not one single piece of unnecessary furniture. She had felt as if she was stepping back in time when she had first walked into this house all that time ago, Sholto's fiancée coming to be introduced to Freddy, his elderly great-uncle.

There was a ripping sound as Sholto widened the tear in her tights to get a better look at her knee. Flinching, her spine pushing into the hard spindles of the chair-back, Molly came alive again, shaken green eyes flying wide on Sholto's downbent dark head. The overhead light gave his thick black hair the iridescent sheen of silk.

'It will hurt when I take the glass out,' he informed her bluntly, sliding fluidly upright again and striding out of the bare little sitting room and into the connecting kitchen.

Molly stared into space, fighting to get a grip on herself again. First things first, that was Sholto. From his aristocratic English mother he had inherited deep reserve, innate practicality and a daunting, chilling self-

discipline. But the other side of his ancestry, like his
spectacular dark good looks, were pure volatile Italian.
Below the ice seethed the fire but she had never ignited
that fire, nor experienced the heat of its flames. His heart
and his beautiful body hadn't burned for her as she'd
burned for him. Rejection, betrayal, unspeakable humiliation…she had experienced them all at his hands.

A long tremor ran through her. He returned with a
bowl of disinfectant, the sharp scent stirring her over-
sensitive stomach. He crossed the room, dominating it
with his sheer size and presence, his every movement
inherently graceful. The silence didn't appear to be both-
ering him. If her descent had shocked him, he had yet
to betray the fact…and how deeply ironic it was that she
had cravenly stayed away from Freddy's funeral to avoid
Sholto only to end up plunging into a far more embarrassing and intimate meeting with him.

In the blink of an eye he had extracted the glass,
cleaned away the blood and fixed a plaster to her cut. A
male who had made pioneering, death-defying trips into
some of the world's most dangerous places would not
find a cut knee much of a challenge. Or the unexpected
arrival of an ex-wife. Molly chewed at her wobbling
lower lip, still white as parchment. But then she had
never been Sholto's wife, not his *real* wife; within a day
of the wedding he had made her a laughing stock in the
world press.

As he sprang upright again, his impassive tawny eyes,
fringed by luxuriant ebony lashes, rested on her. 'I
thought you were a burglar. I'm sorry I gave you a
fright…but do you really have to look at me as if I'm a
cobra about to strike?'

Her lashes fluttered down, delicate colour staining her
cheekbones as her fingers tightened on the chair-arms.
In the background she heard the clink of glass. A tum-

bler was held in front of her. Lifting an unsteady hand, she snatched at it. The brandy hit her aching throat and burned a fiery trail deep into her chilled flesh. Shock; she was still in shock.

'Do you realise that you *still* haven't uttered a single word?' Sholto drawled with controlled impatience.

The tip of her tongue snaked out to moisten her taut lower lip. 'You rather took my breath away...' And as soon as the careless words left her lips her skin flared with such cringing embarrassment, she wanted to sink through the floor. Those had been the exact words she'd used when she'd first told him how much she loved him, rushing to confess what he himself could never have confessed even after he had asked her to marry him. Sholto didn't tell lies but he was a master craftsman at evasion.

'How did you get here? I was asleep but a car pulling in would certainly have awakened me.'

She gulped more of the brandy, trying to be cool about her desperate need for something to settle her jangling nerves. 'My car skidded off the road at the foot of the hill. I walked the rest of the way. I thought Freddy's housekeeper lived in—'

'*Dio*...are you kidding? For thirty-odd years Mrs Mac rode out here every morning on her trusty bicycle. Freddy couldn't have stood anything else. He was fanatical about his privacy. She ate in the kitchen. He ate in here. They only spoke when they had to.'

It was a fuller response than she had expected. She caught the faint roughening of pain in Sholto's deep, dark voice, the Italian accent which thickened only in times of stress, the only barometer she had ever had to what went on deep down inside him. She bowed her head, knowing that aside of Pandora Stevenson the only human being alive who had ever got close to Sholto had been Freddy.

'I rang the doorbell—'

'It hasn't worked for years.'

'I couldn't see a light.'

'There wasn't one on. I assume you've come up here to collect your legacy in person.'

'I told the solicitor I'd come before this but...but something came up.' She stared down at the tattered remnants of her tights, at her exposed knee with its childish plaster, feeling foolish and awkward, the way she so often had in Sholto's radius, and still not quite believing that she was actually here with him. Worse, taking part in a ludicrously inane conversation for two people who had parted in the most violent acrimony and never met face to face again.

'I'm afraid you've had a wasted journey,' Sholto delivered softly, and her head shot up. 'The vase isn't here. It's being delivered to you by courier.'

Colour flooded her cheeks and then receded again, all that went unsaid in that assurance filling her with intense discomfiture. She hadn't come when she had said she would, hadn't bothered to ring in advance, had simply set off from home on an emotion-driven impulse because she had an uneasy conscience.

'You look like death warmed up. I suggest that you take a hot bath,' Sholto murmured.

Molly took the pointed invitation to escape with alacrity and rose in a rush. 'Yes...I'm pretty cold and wet. The bathroom's upstairs, isn't it?'

She staggered slightly and then lurched past him like a fleeing fawn before the hands he put out to steady her could make contact.

'Can you make it up there on your own?' he enquired

in her wake as he switched on the hall light, illuminating the stark narrow staircase with its worn runner.

'Yes...thanks,' she mumbled, and fled.

First left at the top of the stairs. She remembered that, teeth now free to chatter with cold and reaction. She also remembered, before she was married, creeping down-stairs and standing outside the door of Freddy's study, hearing the old man sigh worriedly and say, 'She's as sweet and innocent as a Labrador puppy, Sholto. A country girl with the bloom still on her cheeks. I can see the attraction. But does she have the slightest idea what she's getting into and have you got the patience to stay the course?'

'Not if she listens behind doors like the servants,' Sholto had purred, whipping the door wide to entrap her with burning cheeks and guilty eyes. And he had laughed softly and drawn her forward. 'Answer for your-self, *cara*. Have you the courage to take me on?'

Sholto Cristaldi had been born into one of Italy's most formidable business dynasties. At eighteen he had come into a vast inheritance. She pictured him now, down-stairs, as she ran water into the iron claw-footed bath, her breath misting in the punishingly cold air. Tight black jeans sheathing his long, long legs, a thick cream sweater accentuating his olive-toned skin, luxuriant black hair and magnetic dark eyes. He had the kind of raw physical impact that hit the unwary like a car crash.

What was he doing here in Freddy's bare little house? Sholto had staff to do everything, half a dozen luxurious residences scattered across the globe and a jet-set life-style that came as naturally to him as breathing. Shivering, she removed her damp clothes and sank down into the warm water.

Maybe, if she prayed very, very hard, Sholto would be magically gone when she had finished her bath.

Cowardice, complete cowardice... But she was terrified of exposing her emotions to a male so frighteningly accomplished at concealing his own. She needed to be polite and distant but what she really wanted to do was scream, 'Why did you *do* it? Why did you marry me and then go back to *her*?'

But she was afraid that she already knew why. Afterwards...when it had been all over...only then had she begun to recall and suspect the true meaning of the sly whispers and innuendos that had once gone over her innocent head. Appalled comprehension had come too late, much, much too late for her to protect herself from hurt and harm. Little country girl, naive and blindly trusting and head over heels in love.

With a flying knock, the bathroom door opened and her head jerked round in shock.

'I thought you might appreciate something warm and dry to wear.' With a graceful hand, Sholto cast a couple of folded garments down on the chair by the door.

'Get out!' Molly gasped in horror, whipping protective arms over the embarrassing fullness of her breasts and diving lower in the water, feeling fat and ugly, thinking of Pandora in sudden tearing anguish, slim and slender as a willow wand, without a single ounce of superfluous flesh.

The minute the door closed, Molly scrambled hurriedly out of the bath. Drying herself, she looked in the small mirror above the sink. Tangled hair the colour of autumn leaves fell round her shoulders, framing a heart-shaped face with smudged river-green eyes. Outstandingly ordinary. She was lucky Sholto had recognised her. On their wedding day, she had been rake-thin and her hair had been tinted white-blonde and cut very, very short like a boy's. Living up to Sholto with Pandora's haunting presence in the background had

driven her to strange and increasingly desperate meas-
ures.

His jeans and sweater drowned her five-foot-four-inch
frame. After anchoring the jeans to her waist with the
belt of her skirt, she rolled up the legs several times. The
green sweater fell to her knees. Her shoes were so sod-
den there was no way she could put them on again. She
looked like a refugee from a disaster.

Downstairs, the sitting room was empty. She draped
her damp clothes over a chair-back and set her shoes by
the hearth to dry. From the study next door, she heard
a faint noise like a drawer closing and she went into the
kitchen. A rough board had been wedged into the ap-
erture of the broken window, blocking out the icy blast
of the wind. She set the big kettle on the range. She
would make coffee. That was civilised. She wouldn't let
the hatred and the pain and the bitterness out. She would
match his sublime indifference if it killed her.

But what about her brother, Nigel, and that wretched
loan? Molly grimaced. Four years ago, shortly before
their wedding, Sholto had given Nigel a simply huge
loan. He had used the money to turn their late grandfather's small market garden into a modern garden centre. But late last year her brother had got into debt and
he had fallen behind with the loan. Sholto's bankers had
refused to allow Nigel any more time in which to make
good those missed payments and indeed were now
threatening to repossess both his home and his business.

Until now Molly had been extremely reluctant to
make a direct appeal to Sholto on her brother's behalf.
Nigel was grasping at straws in his naive conviction that
his sister could somehow work a miracle for him and
his family. Molly had had no wish to raise false hopes,
or, if she was honest, to lay her pride on the line for
nothing, for she was certain that Sholto wouldn't pay the

slightest heed to anything she said. However, having found herself under the same roof as Sholto, she knew she wouldn't be able to look her brother in the face again if she didn't at least *try* to persuade Sholto to listen to her.

She pressed the study door open. Sholto was standing looking out of the uncurtained window at the snow, an expression of such grim bleakness etched into his bold, sun-bronzed features that she wished she had left him alone. He studied the beakers on the little tin tray. His wide, sensual mouth hardened, tawny eyes cynically raking her flushed face.

'The answer is *no*,' he breathed with ice-cold clarity.

'I don't know what you're talking about.' But Molly was most terribly afraid that she did and that he was an entire step, if not a complete flight of stairs, ahead of her.

'When you lie, you can't meet my eyes. I used to think that was incredibly sweet.' The cynical laugh he used to crown the admission made her squirm.

Molly's hands shook slightly as she set the tray down on the cluttered Victorian desk that half filled a small room already packed tight with bookshelves and an old swivel chair. Lifting one of the beakers, she turned on her heel.

'Sit down, Molly.' Sholto spun out the swivel chair with deliberate purpose.

She hovered. 'Look, I—'

'Sit down,' he said again, innate authority in every measured syllable.

Molly gave an awkward face-saving shrug. 'OK...fine.'

Sholto braced a lean hip against the edge of the desk and stared down at her, much too close for comfort. 'How did you find out I was here?'

Molly blinked in confusion. 'I hadn't the slightest idea you would be here.'

'Why drive several hundred miles to collect that vase…indeed, why come at all when the solicitor told you that it could be delivered?' Sholto enquired very drily.

Molly dropped her head and stared a hole in the worn rug. 'I wanted to call in at the cemetery and leave some flowers,' she admitted uncomfortably.

The silence stretched.

'I don't believe you, Molly. Your brother has made repeated attempts to contact me. And now, at the eleventh hour, when he is facing repossession, you show up right on my doorstep—'

'*Freddy's* doorstep!' Chagrin and anger combined in her contradiction as she realised where his suspicions lay. 'If you must know, I refused to approach you when Nigel asked me to because I knew it wouldn't do any good and I didn't see why I should make a fool of myself just for your amusement!'

'Go home and tell your brother that he is extremely lucky not to be facing fraud charges,' Sholto delivered with silken emphasis. 'And, believe it or not, he does owe that generosity in part to my former relationship with you.'

Molly leapt up, coffee slopping out of the beaker she still clutched tightly in one hand. '*Fraud?*' she repeated incredulously. 'What on earth are you accusing Nigel of doing?'

Long, sure fingers detached hers from the beaker and set it safely aside. He gazed down at her shocked and angry face and then dense lashes dropped low on his hard, dark eyes.

'Sholto?' Her wary gaze clung to his lean, dark features. Cheekbones to die for were bisected by a fine-boned, aristocratic blade of a nose and matched by a mouth as passionate and wilful as sin. Her heart turned over inside her breast and then beat out a helplessly accelerated tattoo. Almost sick with shame at her response to his sheer animal attraction, she dropped her head again.

'What I'm saying is that when I make a business loan on exceptionally generous terms I don't expect the recipient to plunge a good percentage of the funds I made available into renovating and extending his house and running a top-of-the-range Mercedes!'

Molly's expressive face fell by a mile and slowly she sat down again, seeming to have shrunk in stature even as he spoke. 'But the house is part of the property...and he sold the Merc a couple of months back,' she muttered tautly, uncertainly. 'Was using some of the money that way...fraud?'

'Yes.' The confirmation was level and unemotional. 'As a businessman, Nigel's not a paying proposition and I don't intend to lose any more money on the enterprise. If I chose not to prosecute, it was more for my own benefit than yours. Prosecuting your brother could only have invited the kind of press attention which I most dislike.'

His inhuman cool made her shiver. Molly bit the inside of her lip, a great weariness engulfing her as her thumb absently toyed with Donald's ring, rubbing it as if it might yet be a good-luck talisman. She genuinely hadn't realised that Nigel had misused what was clearly a substantial part of the loan. Nobody had shared that salient and shameful little fact with her.

'I think he must have got carried away...having all that money,' she whispered, and then said with greater force, 'Sholto—?'

'Don't embarrass me, Molly. I have no time for any-

one who tries to rip me off,' he informed her flatly.
'Nigel used that loan as if it was his personal piggybank
and still contrived to run up debts everywhere. If his
problems had resulted from any other cause, I might
have rescheduled the loan, but only a fool throws good
money after bad...and I am not a fool.'

Having absorbed that intimidating tone of absolute fi-
nality, Molly wouldn't have been surprised to discover
that Sholto had just laid her down and walked over her
as if she were a carpet for his arrogant feet; she *felt* as
if he had. Intense mortification filled her. His detachment
was somehow horribly humiliating. They might never
have had a relationship. He seemed to have wiped it out
of his mind as if it had never been.

He had realised their mistake before the ink was dry
on the marriage licence. Desperate to hit back in any
way she could, she had tried to divorce him for adultery.
Instead she had found herself having an annulment
forced on her because their marriage had not been consummated. The tabloid newspapers had had an ecstatic
field day with that titillating revelation. SHOLTO DITCHES
FRIGID BRIDE, had run one unforgettable headline. His
lawyers had chewed her up and spat out her self-esteem
in so many battered pieces.

'When did you get engaged?' Sholto demanded now
with startling abruptness.

Like a woman in a dream, Molly glanced down at the
tiny solitaire still so new and fresh to her finger. It had
belonged to Donald's mother. 'See how you like the feel
of it,' Donald had suggested wryly, neither romance nor
passion having the slightest thing to do with their friendship. But at this moment, quite unbearably, she was recalling another opulent emerald and diamond engagement ring, the one which Sholto had given her, and the
feelings she had had then...her wild excitement, the joy,

the sheer floodtide of love. Her stomach lurching sickly
at the memory, she stood up.

'Where do I sleep?' she asked baldly.

The silence lay as thick and heavy as the blanket of
snow outside.

'Door facing you at the top of the stairs,' Sholto responded in a voice as polished and smooth as silk.

She reached the door.

'Who is he, your fiancé?' he murmured intently.

She didn't turn her head. 'You met him once but you
probably won't remember him. Donald Seaton.'

'Your stepfather's curate?' Sholto gritted in a tone of
explosive incredulity.

'I've known him a long time and he's a very special
person,' Molly retorted, stiff with resentment and bitter
chagrin. 'Goodnight, Sholto. I'll sort out something
about the car first thing in the morning. It's not damaged
but I may need a tow to get it back on the road.'

'*Dio*…you're planning to marry a guy you used to
call Donald Duck?'

Molly yanked the door shut so fast, it closed with a
resounding slam. Donald… He'd been out when she'd
tried to ring him earlier. She should phone him to tell
him where she was. She glanced round the hall. There
was no sign of the telephone she recalled. She checked
the sitting room and then hovered uneasily outside the
study door again. Taking a deep breath and resisting the
temptation to knock, she opened it.

Sholto swung round, shimmering dark eyes alighting
on her in a look as shockingly physical as a ringing slap
across the face. '*Dio mio*…what now?'

Molly was as taken aback by his temper as by his
sudden rudeness. 'I was looking for the phone.'

'Freddy had it disconnected when he went into
hospital.'

'Could I use your mobile?'

Sholto expelled his breath in a slow hiss. 'Who do you have to call?'

'Donald.'

Sholto's hand froze halfway towards the mobile phone lying on the desk and then, with a soft, oddly chilling laugh, he grabbed it up and tossed it carelessly into her hands. 'Be my guest,' he said without any expression at all, and strode out of the room.

Donald answered the phone only after it had rung a dozen times. Molly told him where she was and what had happened. He made soothing sounds.

'Sholto's here too!' The admission exploded out of her with quite unnecessary force.

'I'm glad to hear that you're not up there alone in this weather,' Donald admitted after a brief pause for thought. 'And I imagine a man who's been up Everest can take some snow in his stride! I expect he'll help you with your car too.'

Molly's teeth clenched. 'Somehow I don't see Sholto digging out my car, Donald. Don't you think you're being just a little insensitive?' Her strained voice shook.

'I wish you hadn't asked that question, Molly. I also wish you didn't sound so upset.' Donald sighed. 'It's an overreaction after this length of time. You would be far better occupied mending fences with Sholto.'

'Mending fences?' Molly echoed shrilly.

'Infinitely wiser than continuing to brood and hold spite,' Donald told her with characteristic candour. 'Leave the past where it belongs, Molly. You'll feel a whole lot better if you do, and if you were to make a special effort to forgive Sholto...'

Molly clamped a hand across her mouth like a gag, not trusting herself to speak.

'I expect the concept fills you with horror but I honestly believe that that act of forgiveness would resolve much of what you're feeling right now,' Donald continued with determination. 'Take that extra step, Molly. Ultimately it will bring you the peace of mind you need.'

For the first time ever, Donald had let her down. He did not, *could* not comprehend the torment she was in! To be faced with Sholto again, to be slaughtered by his galling, inhuman indifference—it was ripping her apart. Anger, contempt, hostility she could've borne far more easily—but not his lack of response, which suggested she had been a mere inconvenient hiccup in his life, an aberration swiftly forgotten when he had taken her heart, broken it and somehow held the remains ever since. Poor, foolish, pathetic Molly still hopelessly, obsessively hooked on a male who had branded her with a craving and a need that she still fought with every breath that she drew!

In her flying exit from the study, she almost tripped over Sholto. *'Here!'* she gasped, shoving the mobile phone at him in feverish rejection and then pounding up the stairs two at a time before he could see the tears of rage and self-loathing in her eyes.

CHAPTER TWO

IN A tempest of stormy emotion, Molly switched on the lamp beside the massive Victorian double bed. The bed looked like a ship forcibly squeezed into a too small bottle. The carved mahogany headboard stopped only a foot short of the ceiling and the bed itself was so high, she suspected it enjoyed the benefit of more than one mattress.

A snug little fire glowed in the cast-iron grate on the facing wall. She frowned in surprise, only then noticing the suitcase sitting below the window. How very kind of Sholto to give her the room he had clearly planned to occupy himself! So considerate, so incredibly decent all of a sudden!

Snatching up the case with a shaking hand, she plonked it out on the landing. *Forgive him?* She tore at the jeans, wrenched at the sweater and then slowly, painfully dug her fingers into the garment, bringing it up to her face and breathing in deep. The elusive scent of him engulfed her like a dangerously addictive drug and, hating herself and hating him for being able to exert that evocative power over her even after so long, she flung the sweater aside, horribly ashamed of her lack of control.

Naturally Donald was not worried about her being alone here with Sholto. Sholto might have an exceedingly dangerous reputation with women but Donald and indeed the whole world knew that the one woman Sholto Cristaldi had cheerfully contrived to keep his lustful hands off was Molly! Even when she and Sholto had been engaged he had not made one single serious attempt at seduction.

Deeply humiliated by that awareness, Molly climbed naked into the big bed. She sank into what felt like layer upon layer of feathers. To think that all those years ago she had actually been grateful for what she'd naively seen as Sholto's respectful restraint! But Sholto simply hadn't wanted her enough. And it was also possible, although she cringed at the same suspicion, that all the time he had had another far more satisfying outlet for his sexual needs.

She heard light steps on the stairs, the soft thud of the bathroom door and then she dug her head frantically under the pillow, muffling her ears with two determined hands. Temptation pulled at her and she resisted it. Donald was right. How could she ever go forward if she couldn't overcome this pitiful fascination with a male who had long since given his heart to another woman? And that woman might not be his wife, she might indeed not even be his lover, but she *still* held Sholto more securely than any prison bars of steel.

Molly reared up with a startled squawk as the bedding she had wrapped around her was suddenly wrenched sideways and redistributed. The bedside lamp was on again and momentarily she was blinded by the light. 'What on earth...?'

Her soft mouth fell open as her vision slowly cleared. Sholto reclined like an indolent tiger against the backdrop of the pillows beside her own. The soft glow of the lamp gleamed over wide brown shoulders and powerful pectoral muscles hazed with curling black hair. Something clenched low in her stomach and all of a sudden she felt like someone hurtling down in a runaway lift, made utterly helpless by disbelief and paralysis.

'This is the only bed in the house,' Sholto said softly.

'It…it *can't* be,' Molly whispered weakly.

'Freddy had a horror of visitors who might expect to stay overnight. The other bedroom has not a single stick of furniture,' Sholto informed her, stretching with a long, languorous shifting of limbs. 'Downstairs there are several hard wooden chairs. On a night as cold as this, I am not prepared to sit up until dawn in any one of them.'

Belatedly becoming conscious that she was exposing a rather bountiful amount of bosom. Molly snatched the linen sheet all the way to her shoulders. 'You're not sharing this bed with me!'

An ebony brow climbed. 'Now why is it that I am experiencing a strong sense of *déjà vu*?'

Thoroughly unnerved by that leading question, Molly felt the burn as a slow, painful flush of appalled comprehension crawled up her throat.

'*Sì*…I have it now…the wedding night we never had,' Sholto supplied for himself in the same considering tone from which any hint of emotion had been ruthlessly erased. 'All those weeks and weeks of anticipation and then? *Nothing*…Something of an anticlimax, *cara*.'

Molly's heart sank like a concrete block inside her. In an involuntary flash she recalled that night, his murderously quiet but cold fury when she had tried to lock him out of the bedroom, her hysterical anger and tears. In a sharp, defensive movement, she turned her head away, fiercely burying the memory deep and shutting it back out of her mind again.

'If you turn your back, I'll get up and get dressed again. I have no objection to spending the night in a chair,' she stated stiffly, hoping to shame him into making that move himself.

'Turn my *back*?' Sholto repeated with flaring incredulity. 'Molly, are you fifteen or twenty-four?'

As her cheeks flared with fresh embarrassment, she

cursed her fair skin and set her teeth together. 'I'm not wearing anything.'

'Neither am I but I am not so overcome by conceit that I imagine that one flash of my unclothed body will incite you to insatiable lust.'

'Don't make fun of me!' she bit out tautly.

'*Dio, cara...*' Sholto purred like a big, indolent cat basking at his leisure in the sunshine. 'Are you afraid that I might not be able to control myself if I have a glimpse of naked female flesh?'

'Of course not but—'

'Then what are you worried about?'

Molly's fingers tightened on the bedding. 'We can't possibly sleep in the same bed. It wouldn't be right.'

'Who's going to know?' Sholto prompted very drily.

'*I would know!* That's not the point. The point is—'

'That you're the most frightfully stuffy little prig and you ought to be ashamed of yourself. What do you think I'm going to do...jump you as soon as the light goes out?'

Sick with mortification, Molly dragged her stricken gaze from glittering eyes that shone pure lambent gold. 'No.'

'Or maybe it's yourself that you don't trust. Am I the one in danger?' Sholto enquired even more drily.

'Don't be ridiculous.' Molly found herself sinking back below the bedding by slow, almost involuntary degrees until the back of her head rested on the pillows again. Abruptly the blankets at his side of the bed were thrust back. Out of the corner of her eye, she glimpsed his long, golden-skinned back view as he sprang out of bed. The door opened. She rolled over, feverishly grateful that he was leaving, and then, suddenly, without any warning whatsoever, desperately disappointed. She shut her eyes tightly, fearfully aware that she was no longer in control of her own emotional reactions.

A soft bundle of cloth landed beside her cheek. 'What—?'

'A T-shirt, *cara*...and I'll put on something too, shall I?' Sholto proffered with deeply sardonic bite.

It was an unexpected compromise and not one she should accept. But the prospect of sitting blue with cold for hours on end in that cheerless ice-box of a room downstairs was far from tempting. She snatched the garment below the covers, rustled about like a hamster burrowing into cotton wool and pulled the T-shirt over her head, smoothing it down over her hips with careful hands. The bed shifted as Sholto's weight came down on it again. Molly lay rigid as a marble pillar, knowing that every scrap of common sense she possessed urged retreat but somehow not flexing a toe to leave the bed, even though she *was* now decently covered.

A prig. Well, yes, she probably was. The accusation stung but, in all honesty, could not be denied.

She had no memory of her own father. He had died when she was a baby and her mother had married the Reverend George Gilpin two years later. Her stepfather had been a strict disciplinarian with a cold puritanical outlook. Molly had been raised in a stiflingly inhibited household where any display of naked flesh was viewed as indecent and where any reference to the physical intimacy between a man and a woman was joylessly linked only to procreation and the married state.

Sholto had no such inhibitions but then he had not been introduced to the facts of life by a mother who had clearly considered the whole process pretty disgusting. Nor had he been told that it was a woman's duty just to put up with what she didn't like. And when Molly had once foolishly blurted out that it felt like heaven to be in Sholto's arms her late mother had surveyed her with distaste and had implied that she would find nothing heavenly about the ultimate act of intimacy.

Uneasy with the sexual tenor of her thoughts, Molly turned over on her side, trying very hard not to be aware of the perceptible heat emanating from the large male frame lying very little distance from her. It was like a test, she told herself bracingly—a test of whether or not she had grown at all since that annulment. Sholto had once seemed the answer to every adolescent prayer she had ever had and she had behaved like a starstruck teenager until the hurt and the humiliation had come and woken her up to hard reality.

Yet she had still never managed to forget him. Memories haunted her—*he* haunted her. The nagging sense of bitter loss still lingered. Yet what had she actually lost? Their entire relationship had been a cruel charade. So how could she still be attracted to him? His looks had a lot to do with it, she told herself in growing desperation. It was incredibly hard to be indifferent to a drop-dead gorgeous male whom you had once passionately loved.

Sholto shifted in a restive movement and she tensed, feeling the dangerous valley in the centre of the mattress beckoning and clinging with grim death to the safe slope on her side.

'There's just you and me and a blizzard outside,' he murmured in an almost savouring tone.

She supposed he was enjoying even the small challenge provided by the bad weather. He would've relished the challenge of staying alive out in the blizzard even more. Freddy had once told her that Sholto had a great need to prove himself in taxing physical environments because only in that field could he find a genuine challenge and yet start level and equal with other men.

So Sholto had gone deep-sea diving in shark-infested waters, conquered mountains and travelled deep into the jungles of Indonesia on scientific expeditions, his restive vitality finding an outlet in exploration and discovery from an early age. But then that was what he did for amusement, light relief from the even tougher challenge of keeping Cristaldi Investments Inc. at the top of the international money league. That was why, the more she thought about it, it was all the more extraordinary to find Sholto in the wintry depths of the Lake District apparently doing nothing.

'What are you doing up here?' she suddenly whispered, opening her eyes to see the flames of the fire dancing shadows on the walls and ceiling, making the room unexpectedly light and bright.

'Freddy left half a century of family correspondence for me to sort out and I wanted to see the place one last time before I sold it.'

Molly thrust her cheek into the pillow, wishing she hadn't opened a conversation, wishing she could just fall asleep.

'And now, for your sake, I'm very glad that I did,' Sholto added with silken emphasis.

'*My* sake?' she queried, wondering if she had heard him right.

'You're making a very big mistake with Donald.'

Disconcerted and then inflamed by that cool, measured assurance, Molly flopped flat and stared up at the ceiling, her tension pronounced. 'You don't know him and it's none of—'

'He'll complete the job your mother and your step-father started. You'll be baking buns and smiling when you feel like screaming for the rest of your days…that is if you don't end up cracking up under the strain of living a lie because you're not in love with him.'

Molly breathed in so deep, it felt as if she had a balloon inflating inside her lungs. 'How the heck would *you* know?' she splintered before she could swallow back the outraged demand and contrive a calmer response.

'Who would know better?' Sholto drawled with galling cool. 'You were crazy about me once. All seething, heaving passion, jealousy and possessiveness...the whole lot quivering like a stick of dynamite waiting for a match beneath that deceptively quiet surface of yours. Dangerously volatile but with considerable promise of excitement, I used to think.'

'How dare you talk about me like that?' Her voice shook with incredulous censure as she lifted herself up on one elbow.

'Careful,' Sholto warned lazily, brilliant eyes arrowing over her flushed and furious face before skimming down to the T-shirt which was falling off one slim shoulder. 'You are revealing bare skin...'

Sitting up in one driven motion, Molly snatched at the recalcitrant neckline and hauled it up again. 'I am extremely fond of Donald.'

'It'll take more than that to sustain a marriage. Still, I expect your stepfather approves. He'll be in his element with a son-in-law he can patronise and bully.'

'Just because he didn't like *you*—'

'Donald's far too old for you and he can't have the slightest idea of what you're really like.'

'Stop talking about me as if I'm some sort of freak!' Molly blazed back at him, her hands knotting into fists. 'I trust Donald. I know him! He'll never, ever let me down or deceive me.'

'And I *did*? Is that what you think?'

Molly froze as if he had slapped her, face falling, stark vulnerability etched in her wide green eyes. The silence pounded. It was like being trapped inside a dark tunnel, hearing the threatening thunder of an approaching train. Unwarily, she clashed with Sholto's blazing golden look of challenge and her throat closed over, stomach twisting sickly.

Lowering her lashes, she blocked him out. Somehow they had strayed into very dangerous territory. Wary now, petrified of betraying the extent of her emotional turmoil, she started to lie down again, every nerve jangling. 'I'm tired...I'm going to sleep.'

'You think I'm about to say "Goodnight and sweet dreams"?' Sholto slid across the bed, closing the gap between them in one smooth, purposeful movement. 'Listen to yourself. You're talking like a painfully well brought up little girl at a rowdy pyjama party.'

'Sholto...this stupid argument has gone far enough.'

A scorching smile flashed across his savagely handsome features as he looked down at her anxious face. A teasing forefinger slowly spiralled into the tumbled strands of gleaming russet hair spilling across the pillow. 'But I haven't even begun yet, *cara*.'

Molly blinked up at him in complete bemusement. That devastating smile that squeezed her heart tight, so rare and once so precious, the playful fingers toying with her hair... Rational thought blurred, her breath shortening in her throat.

'Begun what?' She stared up at him in bewildered enquiry.

'If you've forgotten what it was like between *us*, you need a reminder,' Sholto spelt out softly as he lowered his dark, arrogant head.

Her brow furrowed in confusion, her uncertain eyes locking with his. He had spectacular eyes, deep-set and dark gold, spiked by dense black lashes, and the intensity of that smouldering gaze held her entrapped. She could not believe he was going to kiss her for why should he do such a thing? And then he *did*. That wide, sensual mouth slowly drifted down onto hers like something out of a dream, so that when he took her softly parted lips and let the tip of his tongue slide erotically between them she was without defence and utterly unprepared for the devastating charge of excitement that engulfed her.

In shock, she meant to push him away. Her hand lifted and braced against a broad, muscular shoulder that was smooth as satin but infinitely more tactile and tempting. For an instant her mind warred with her body, telling her no...no, not right, not allowed...yet her fingers only flexed against that warm brown skin, touching, almost clenching into a move of denial but somehow not quite making it. And as quickly that moment of choice and awareness was lost. For Molly, time had stopped dead in its tracks and gone into reverse.

He slid a strong arm beneath her and lifted her up to him to let his tongue drive deep between her lips in passionate demand. A shaken gasp was torn from her as he made love to her mouth with wicked, wild expertise, ruthlessly ravishing the sensitive interior until she was hot and dizzy and clutching at him, her blood pounding terrifyingly fast in her veins.

'No comparison, is there, *cara*?' A husky, almost chilling laugh sent a responsive shiver down her spine but all she knew was that it was heaven to be in his arms again, shy fingers free to dart into the luxuriant black silk of his hair where it grew low and slightly too long at the nape of his neck.

'Sholto...?' she muttered unevenly, her mind struggling to get a grip.

His hand moved against the firm curve of her breast, which was shielded only by the fine cotton. Her eyes squeezed shut as her nipples peaked into hard, aching little buds, depriving her of breath and voice simultaneously. Repossessing her mouth with passionate hunger, he hooked long fingers deftly into the wide neckline of the T-shirt and tugged it down out of his path.

As his sure hands shaped her swelling breasts, a kind of exquisite agony consumed Molly. His thumbs flicked over the taut peaks, making her strain up to him and moan in shock at the power of that sensation. His mouth followed the slender, arching column of her throat, lingered to toy with racing pulse-points and traced a teasing path of hot, darting kisses over her quivering flesh before capturing an urgently sensitive pink crest with ruthless deliberation. She cried out, then fought just to breathe, heart hammering at an insane rate as her fingers bit fiercely into his shoulders.

His tongue swirled and teased with erotic expertise and then he nipped the taut, swollen tip with his teeth, hotly suckling while she writhed and whimpered, shock piling on sensual shock to overwhelm her. Liquid fire flared and burned unbearably between her trembling thighs. As he shifted his long, lithe body to mete out the same treatment to the other pouting peak, he parted her shivering legs with his knee and gently pinned her down.

'Dio...you have the most exquisitely sexy body,' Sholto intoned thickly, sinking appreciative hands beneath the generous curve of her hips and plundering her lips afresh.

When lean fingers skimmed through the damp tangle of chestnut curls guarding the apex of her thighs she went rigid and then gasped out loud and writhed as he found her secret place. Frantic heat flashed through her and then centred on the pulsing ache at the very heart of her. Wildly out of control from that moment on, she twisted helplessly in passion's thrall, tormented by sensation and choking, blinding waves of ever heightening excitement.

Sholto pressed her down and spread her beneath him when she was at a mindless, wordless peak of intolerable arousal. For a split second, he hesitated and her eyes opened, catching the raw satisfaction stamped in his darkly flushed features before he pushed back her thighs and entered her with a single driving thrust. Pain and pleasure linked as she cried out in bitter-sweet shock at that powerful invasion and he covered her mouth fiercely with his again in a stormy brand of possession.

It was wild; it was like nothing she had ever imagined. Overwhelming hunger and need clawed at her even in the wake of that stabbing pain. She wanted, needed, *craved* every urgently sexual move of his hot, hard, demanding body on hers. She was flying up into the sun, every fibre of her being ablaze with screaming desperation. He plunged into her faster and faster, forcing her higher and higher until the fierce heat and the even fiercer ache collided deep inside her and sent her sobbing and shuddering into an explosive release.

The world was still spinning when she opened her eyes again. A daze of unfamiliar languorous contentment kept her limp and still. Sholto's arms were still tight around her, his big, powerful body damp and heavy on hers. He lifted his tousled dark head and stared down at her, not a muscle moving on his lean, dark face, brilliant eyes impenetrable.

'Thanks,' he drawled without any expression at all. 'You were everything I ever hoped you would be.'

CHAPTER THREE

IN ONE lithe movement, Sholto released Molly from his weight and sprang out of bed. Utterly unselfconscious, he stretched, firelight gleaming over his damp golden skin and playing over the whipcord muscles flexing in his back. In the thunderous silence, he pulled on a pair of black briefs and reached for his jeans with complete cool.

Molly sat up with an uncoordinated jerk and stared. Uncertainly, she cleared her dry throat. 'Sholto...?'

'I'll take the chair downstairs now,' he told her as he yanked up the zip on his jeans with a fluid twist of his lean hips.

'What...?' It was a dulled whisper of incomprehension. Molly was in too much turmoil to be able to reason with any clarity.

Sholto slid his arms into a silk shirt, buttoned it with deft fingers and tugged on a black sweater. Then he strolled to the end of the bed and curved lean, strong hands round the ornate footboard. He surveyed her rigid figure in the centre of the tangled bedding, his attention lingering on her wildly mussed hair, dazed eyes and swollen pink mouth. '*Dio*...I've waited a long time to see you like this,' he confided softly.

This time Molly felt his cold menace. It was like the diamond-bright glitter of icy snow crystals freezing her shrinking flesh.

'And you made it so damned easy for me, I should be ashamed of myself for taking advantage of a trusting virgin...but I'm *not* ashamed,' Sholto asserted without a flicker of conscience as he watched her face slowly drain of colour. 'I paid for that pleasure four years ago when I married you. Do you actually recall that wedding ceremony, Molly? Do you even remember the promises you made then? And do you also recall packing your bags that same night and running home to hide behind your parents?'

Molly was shaking, still so much in shock at what she had allowed to happen between them that she could barely credit that there could be even worse to come. 'A-are you saying,' she framed jerkily. 'th-that you deliberately chose to make love to me?'

'Lovemaking is what you would have had on our wedding night,' Sholto responded with sardonic bite. 'Tonight you had sex.'

Cringing from that demeaning description of their intimacy and in no state to guard her speech, Molly muttered shakily, 'I thought you got carried away...like I did.'

An unexpected and very faint suggestion of colour briefly accentuated the slant of Sholto's hard cheekbones but a cynical black brow flared. 'Do you really think that's likely?'

A deep dark flush scored her cheeks. She hunched her shoulders over her raised knees, her stomach churning. How could she have imagined for one moment that Sholto could have been responding to *her* non-existent sex appeal? And, of course, a male of his experience didn't simply surrender to temptation and lose control like an impetuous, unthinking teenager. But the mere idea that Sholto had climbed with cold-blooded calculation into the bed for the express and sole purpose of depriving her of her virginity made Molly feel sick and incredibly degraded.

'I don't understand,' she confessed unevenly, clasping

her trembling hands round her knees, not wanting to understand but knowing that she needed to know why, *why* and on what possible grounds Sholto should have decided that she deserved such a retribution.

She watched his long, beautifully shaped fingers flex on the footboard, the knuckles briefly showing the white of bone through the brown skin. 'I find it incredible that you shouldn't understand,' he admitted, his Italian accent roughening his vowel sounds. 'Now where do I start? Perhaps the desire for revenge was born when I found myself being threatened by the police for trying to approach my runaway wife.'

'The *police*?' she echoed, her head shooting up again in astonishment.

'Your stepfather called them. I was warned off for causing a public disturbance. Now I don't believe it was my fault that the paparazzi were encamped outside your parents' house or that they went crazy when I arrived...but somehow I received the blame.' The chill of his accusing appraisal, the hardening of his strong facial bones told her how outraged he had been by the experience.

Molly had known about that visit he had made but she hadn't known about the interference of the police. Dismay on his behalf briefly assailed her. No, that hadn't been fair but physical force wouldn't have persuaded her to see him then and, in any case, she hadn't been staying with her parents at the time. She had known better than to turn to her stepfather or her mother for sympathy when her marriage had gone so horrendously and publicly wrong.

'The desire for revenge might well have died a natural death once I came to the conclusion that I had had a lucky escape,' Sholto continued with brutal candour.

'But it was what you did to my cousin, Pandora, that I could never forgive or forget.'

'Pandora?' Molly breathed in a sick undertone, barely able to get her vocal cords round that name.

'The Press tore her apart. She was tied to the stake by the tabloids and burned like a witch. People cut her dead; friends stopped calling. She was even spat at in the street,' Sholto recited grittily. 'Pandora, the man-hungry, promiscuous bitch, who supposedly stole the groom from Molly, the poor martyred little bride...that's how she was portrayed. And why did that happen? Because *you* told a bunch of filthy lies to a journalist!'

'I didn't!' Molly protested, a choking sob building in her throat, but she turned her head away even as she said it. She hadn't been the one to do the talking but she knew who had. Outraged on her behalf, Jenna, her then best friend, had passed on her indiscreet confidences about Molly and Sholto to an eager reporter. Molly hadn't given Jenna permission to do that, nor would she have, but she could not deny that at the time she had experienced a bitter satisfaction when Pandora was vilified by the Press for her role in the break-up of their marriage.

'You let loose the whole media circus,' Sholto condemned, swinging restively away from the bed.

'No, you did that,' Molly contradicted him, her voice low and tremulous as she bowed her pounding head over her knees. 'You did that when you were photographed leaving Pandora's apartment at dawn the day after our wedding.'

'You were my wife. I had the right to expect *some* degree of trust and loyalty from you,' Sholto drawled with chilling bite from the fireplace.

She could barely absorb what he was telling her because he had utterly devastated her with the cruel reality of what had lain behind his seduction. Molly had never really accepted that Sholto could be as ruthless as he had always been painted and only now did she appreciate that in the years since the annulment she had learnt to partially excuse him for the terrible pain he had caused her. Somewhere in the back of her mind she had begun to believe that he might well have married her in a desperate, possibly even praiseworthy attempt to break off his relationship with Pandora, but that he had ultimately found himself unable to sustain such a deception when Pandora had refused to let go.

'You got what you deserved,' she murmured painfully. 'Exactly what you deserved. I used to think that maybe you couldn't help yourself and now you've taught me differently. I did trust you and that was stupid but I would rather go through life being stupid than become a cold, unfeeling—'

'*Dio*...never, ever unfeeling,' Sholto interposed with silken emphasis from the door. 'But revenge is a dish best eaten cold and I really could not stomach the idea of you marrying Donald and producing a host of little portly, pigeon-toed children. What did that clod do to deserve *my* wedding night? Well, if he takes you now, *cara*, let him do so knowing that you were mine first!'

Molly shuddered with appalled distaste. Sholto gazed back at her, golden eyes ablaze with challenge. He was quite unashamed of the primitive sentiments he had just expressed. And that was yet another revelation to Molly. Four years ago, she had married an unprincipled savage without knowing it, indeed had fondly believed that Sholto was the very last word in laid-back cool and control.

As the door closed she stared into the smouldering heart of the fire, conscious of the shadows now gathering in the corners. The flames had died down like the counterfeit passion and soon there would be nothing left but ashes. Sholto was a prince of deception and he had run rings round her with his sexual charisma. He had done it in the name of revenge and suddenly Molly was desperately grateful that she did not love Donald and that he did not love her.

Donald would be disappointed but not hurt when she returned his ring. He had only proposed at the weekend and he had urged her to think very, very carefully before she gave him her final answer. She had lain awake last night and then had put on the ring when she got up, resolving to tell Donald of her decision when she returned from this trip. But that now seemed a lifetime ago and Sholto had just smashed what she might have had with Donald. She was deeply ashamed of her own physical weakness. A woman who could so easily and foolishly succumb to the sexual allure of one man had no business at all even considering a serious relationship with another.

A cheap one-night stand. That was what she had made of herself. He had even dared to censure her for what Pandora had suffered! But then, albeit unwittingly, she had attacked and hurt the woman he loved. Indeed, tonight Sholto had taught her what real hatred was and it was not the weak illusion that she had hidden behind to conserve her own pride. But she still found it incredible that Sholto could blame her for their broken marriage, could question *her* loyalty and trust. For, hysterical or not on their wedding night, she had made her feelings quite clear...

'If you go to her, I won't be here when you come back!' she had told him, shooting the last bolt on her pride with that ultimatum because she had not been able to credit, had not been able to *believe* until he'd actually walked out the door that any male would leave a sobbing and already distraught bride to go to another woman on his wedding night.

And Sholto had made his choice. Indeed, Sholto had made his choice without hesitation. If he had come in search of her afterwards…well, it had already been too late. When Molly had seen that photo of him emerging from Pandora's apartment block at dawn, had been faced with the humiliating public proof that he had spent the whole night with his cousin, she had never wanted to set eyes on Sholto again. The agony of that betrayal had been too immense.

And yet they had started out with such apparent promise, she conceded painfully, struggling not to let the memories flood back, for the last thing she needed now was to wallow in the distant past. But somehow the temptation to recall a happier time was irresistible.

She had first met Sholto on one of those hot, still summer afternoons when anything physical felt like an outrageous effort. She had been coasting her bike down the hill, her basket full of eggs from the village shop, when a black sports car had suddenly shot out of a leafy lane in front of her. Her frantic evasive manoeuvres had sent her flying head first into the hedge. When the world had righted itself again, Sholto had got out of the car and was helping her disentangle herself from the brambles, exclaiming about the scratches on her bare arms and apologising.

A languid female voice had drifted from the sports car. 'Ask her where the Hendersons live…'

Sholto had stridden back to the car and wrenched open the driver's door. After a terse exchange, a tall, beautiful blonde with a sullen mouth had reluctantly emerged. 'I'm sorry you came off your bike but you really should've been looking where you were going—'

'You were driving like a bat out of hell,' Sholto interposed, looking at the blonde with icy reproof.

For an instant Sholto and Pandora stood side by side, and together, as Molly got her first really good look at them, they took her breath away. One so dark and one so fair and both of them possessed of that compelling kind of physical beauty which turned heads and fascinated. Never had Molly been more horribly conscious of a face bare of make-up, hair tangled by the breeze and a faded summer dress that had seen better days.

'The Hendersons,' Pandora repeated impatiently.

'You'll have to excuse my cousin, Pandora. She's not very good with strangers,' Sholto murmured wryly as he extended a lean hand to Molly. 'Sholto Cristaldi. Where were you heading when we interrupted your journey?'

'Home.' Her uncertain gaze collided with shimmering dark golden eyes as she clasped his hand. And he didn't let go again. He kept on holding her hand, a faint frown-line etched between his aristocratic brows as he stared intently down at her until a deep flush of self-consciousness coloured her cheeks and she tugged her own fingers clumsily free.

'Sholto, we're *late*!' Pandora snapped.

'What's your name?' Sholto asked, as if his cousin had neither spoken nor even existed.

'Molly...Molly Bannister.'

'Molly,' he repeated softly, his slow, utterly devastating smile flashing out to leave her weak at the knees. While he crouched down over her bike, examining the bent wheel and the messy debris of broken eggs, she just stared down at him in complete fascination, feverishly, childishly wishing that she had legs that ran all the way up to her armpits, smaller breasts, slimmer hips and last but not least a face that would launch a thousand ships.

In short she would've sold her soul at that moment to

have the looks to attract a male of Sholto's calibre. But she had no expectation of such a miracle taking place. Sholto, with his lazy, well-bred drawl, supreme sophistication and exquisitely cut casual clothes, had all the glamour of a film star and seemed just as unattainable.

'I think the first thing we need to do is replace the eggs,' Sholto stated with deadly seriousness as he sprang lithely upright again.

'Give her some money for them, for heaven's sake!' Pandora urged incredulously.

'You don't need to replace them,' Molly said hurriedly. 'And I certainly don't want any money—'

'And then we need to take you and your bike home,' Sholto continued smoothly, as good at ignoring Molly's objections as he apparently was at blocking out the increasingly angry interruptions coming from his cousin. 'Where *do* the Hendersons live?'

'You go up the hill, through the village and about a hundred yards further on there's a big set of gates on the left—'

'We'll drop my cousin off first…since she's in such a hurry,' Sholto murmured softly. 'But I'm afraid you'll find it a frightful squeeze in what passes for a back seat in this car.'

'I don't need a lift… I wouldn't dream of it. I can *walk* home from here!' she gabbled in a rush, hideously conscious of Pandora's outraged stare at the idea of her even getting into their car.

But Sholto won out. Taking charge of the steering wheel, he dropped his cousin off at the Hendersons' Edwardian mansion and ushered Molly into the passenger seat in her stead.

'Explain that we had an accident and offer my apologies,' he instructed a frozenly furious Pandora.

Then he drove Molly back to the village shop, replaced the eggs, parked the car beside her damaged bike and proceeded to walk her and the bike home to the vicarage. It was a mile-long walk and she wished it were five miles longer. Sholto and Pandora had been invited to what he called a 'house party' at the Hendersons' and Molly tried to behave as if she regularly met people who just flew in from New York on Concorde and drove down to the country in a flashy sports car for the weekend.

She never expected to see him again after he parted from her at the vicarage gates. She was astonished when his hostess phoned that evening and asked her if she would like to come up and play tennis the following afternoon. Although the Hendersons allowed the annual church fête to be held in the grounds of their impressive home, they were not in the habit of inviting their more humble neighbours to socialise with them.

Molly knew that she could only owe that invitation to Sholto. Indeed, he carelessly confirmed the fact when he came to pick her up. She was less comfortable with the admission when she witnessed the extraordinary deference shown to him by his hosts.

The haughty Hendersons fawned on Sholto as if he were visiting royalty and Sholto did not appear to notice anything amiss in their excessive eagerness to please. That he was accustomed to that sort of attention was obvious but his manners were faultless and that day Molly was blissfully ignorant both of Sholto's immense wealth and of the way that same wealth could affect other people.

It was far too hot for tennis but the heat didn't bother Sholto, so nobody dared to complain. Molly ran herself into the ground during a very athletic game of mixed doubles and thoroughly enjoyed herself until she saw her reflection in a window afterwards and cringed at the sight of her wet hair, shiny nose and hot cheeks. Sholto paused behind her, even then able to read her like a book. 'You look gorgeous, *cara*. Women who think of nothing but their appearance are very poor company.'

Cousin Pandora spent the afternoon sitting cool as a cucumber on the sidelines and flirting like mad with two different men. She barely looked at Molly but Molly had already realised that Pandora had little time for her own sex. Only the day before she had seen Sholto treat Pandora like a spoilt and wilful kid sister. At that stage, she didn't see the other woman as even a cloud on her horizon…and she was utterly overwhelmed by Sholto's apparent interest in her…

Molly woke with a start. The events of the previous night flooded back and she could not believe that she had actually slept. It was already after ten. Scrambling out of bed, she pulled back the curtains. Some time during the night she had heard driving rain lash the window. It was no longer raining and the snow had gone as quickly as it had come.

The skirt and sweater which she had left downstairs now lay on the chair, and with them a new pair of black tights. Where had Sholto got the tights from? She recalled the shop at the garage where she had stopped for petrol the night before. She stiffened at the awareness that he had entered the room while she slept but she was grateful not to be forced to go downstairs in *his* clothes.

Crossing the landing to the bathroom, she ran a shallow bath. She told herself that it was her imagination telling her that she could still smell Sholto on her skin. Imagination and guilt, she reflected painfully, lathering herself with soap and wishing she could as easily wash away the incredibly intimate ache she could still feel, the starkly unavoidable reminder of his possession.

Suddenly she froze in dismay. Had he taken any precautions? Had he protected her...wasn't that the expression? As quickly she scolded herself for her naive attack of panic. *Of course* Sholto would've ensured that his calculated seduction didn't result in a pregnancy. Obviously that would be the very last thing he would've risked. That she didn't recall any evidence of the fact meant nothing. Her teeth gritted. Wantonly and mindlessly lost in the grip of intense physical excitement, she had been far beyond such powers of common sense and observation.

At the top of the stairs some ten minutes later, she snatched in a deep, steadying breath and threw back her shoulders. As she descended Sholto emerged from the sitting room. Molly fixed her attention rigidly to a point slightly to the left of him.

'Would you like some breakfast?' he enquired.

The offer was sufficiently startling to surprise her into looking directly at him. But the terribly tearing pain she had feared failed to materialise. She felt numb and empty, temporarily drained by the self-castigating and bitter regrets of the night.

'We should talk, Molly.'

'The one thing I will not do is talk to you,' Molly said tightly, and stepped past him.

She hadn't eaten since teatime the night before. It surprised her that in the midst of everything she could experience such fierce hunger pangs. In the kitchen, she put on the kettle. A packet of chocolate-filled croissants lay on the counter. Sholto adored chocolate. It was one of the little things about him that she had loved most. As she removed her strained gaze from the sight, she saw a glimmer of familiar red through the opaque glass pane in the back door.

The door open, she stared at her elderly hatchback. 'How did my car get up here?'

'The back wheels were bogged down in the mud,' Sholto supplied. 'I towed it out.'

'What with?'

'I came up here in a four-wheel drive. You didn't see it because it was in the garage…and your car keys were in your jacket,' Sholto reminded her.

Molly turned away again. She could not bear to thank him after what he had done to her. Their intimacy had not been accidental, had not been brought about by a sudden attack of lust or sentimentality on his part or even a loss of control. He had chosen his revenge with cruel deliberation. In silence, she ripped open the packet of croissants to put one into the oven to heat. Pride would not allow her to make a fleeing, craven retreat even if her car was conveniently waiting at the door. But no doubt he would be glad to see her go.

Lost in her own disjointed thoughts, she was staring blankly at the tiled wall when Sholto strode past her to take the kettle off the boil. He flipped the slightly singed croissant out of the oven with a deft hand. 'You're upset. Sit down. I'll make the coffee.'

'I am not upset.' But she was shivering with cold and she wrapped her arms round herself tightly. In one lithe, disturbing movement, Sholto peeled off his sweater and extended it to her, brilliant dark eyes intent on her drawn profile. Molly surveyed the garment with revulsion and backed away into the sitting room to sink down at the table.

The croissant turned to dust in her mouth and she had to force it down. Her appetite had mysteriously vanished. She found herself stealing furtive, bewildered glances at Sholto. He had brought up her clothes, replaced her torn tights and retrieved her car. But then each and every one of those attentions would also speed her departure and the effortless good manners and the innate sophistication of a male who knew her sex were back in full play again. Last night might never have happened.

Yet last night Sholto had revealed more emotion than she had ever dreamt he might possess on the subject of their marriage. And there was a taut, gritty edge to his spectacular bone structure now, a tightness in the set of his hard mouth that betrayed his continuing tension. The silence smouldered and she was no more at ease with it than he was. Pushing back her plate, she stood up and stretched out her hand towards her jacket.

'I wasn't planning to touch you when I got into that bed,' Sholto drawled softly.

Her hand fell back from her jacket, her face filling with mortified colour. 'A wicked impulse, was it…a bit of a joke?' she heard herself bite back with a bitterness that shook her. 'As much of a sick joke as our marriage?'

Sholto stilled, briefly disconcerted by her sarcasm, and then he strode closer and Molly spread her arms wide in a gesture of angry warning. 'Don't you dare come near me!'

'Hit me if it makes you feel better.' Tawny eyes watched her with formidably controlled intensity.

Molly didn't want to do anything that *he* wanted her to do. She wouldn't let herself lash out and shatter the last, torturously thin shreds of her control. She drew her arms in again, tight to her sides like a little tin soldier who had broken the line and earned a reproof.

'When I kissed you, it was a game…I didn't intend to let it go so far,' Sholto confessed with a grim edge to his deep, dark drawl, but Molly had already turned her back on him in self-defence.

A game? That precious, wonderful numbness was gone now when she most needed it. Trick or treat, tease and withdraw. Only Sholto had not withdrawn, Sholto had discovered that the response he could gain from his once reluctant bride was more than equal to anything he had been able to extract when she had been in love with him. Had that tantalised him, amused him into continuing his cruel and sadistic game?

'*Dio…*' he gritted, his accent an unbearably sexy purr round the syllables. 'I really wanted you.'

'I feel so much better knowing that.' He had *really* wanted her. What did that mean and couldn't he even have had the decency to conceal the vein of surprise that was audible in that admission?

And she wasn't stupid. Did he have to talk to her as if she were? Sexual desire wasn't an intellectual thing. Her abandoned response had aroused him and after that it had simply been a question of male lust. She didn't need that reality spelt out. But Sholto had known exactly what he was doing. He hadn't stopped because he hadn't seen why he should. And she would be a very old lady before she forgot his look of savage satisfaction at the instant he had invaded her writhing body with his.

'And you wanted me,' Sholto stated with cool and complete conviction.

Molly froze, shock shrilling through her.

'Nor do I recall employing any undue persuasion,' Sholto drawled in smoothly provocative continuance. 'In fact if you hadn't been with me every eager step of the way it would never have happened.'

Molly spun round so fast, she stumbled, but her open palm still cracked across one hard cheekbone with stinging force. Then she staggered back a step, devastated by the violence that had betrayed her and smashed her control.

'I didn't want you…and I want nothing more to do with you…*ever*!' she stressed, clashing with glittering golden eyes that were as cold as ice. For a split second, she couldn't break the compelling hold of that scrutiny and that panicked her even more. Then, snatching up her things, she headed for the back door at speed.

She was shaking like a leaf when she got behind the steering wheel but she drove off with exaggerated care, taking the hill which had caused her such grief the night before like a learner driver. Then she noticed the flowers still lying on the passenger seat, the bouquet for Freddy which she had intended to leave at the cemetery. The little church was only a couple of miles further down the road. She performed the task, indifferent to the rain that had come on again.

'He's too proud and too angry to chase after you,' Freddy had written in an urgent letter to her after all that grotesque publicity about the marriage split. 'If you want Sholto back, the first move will have to be yours...'

And she had responded to him with a whole tissue of face-saving lies. Freddy had deserved better. Weeks and weeks later, she had sat down and written again. It had been a kind of catharsis telling Freddy that love wasn't always enough and that she could never, ever have lived with being second best.

'It *is* a rather elegant shape,' Donald conceded as he set the graceful, slender-necked vase back on the shelf. 'But it's a shame that it's not that lovely shade of blue which the Chinese were so clever with. Do you think you ought to have it valued?'

'No...I love it but I shouldn't think it's worth much. I admired it the first time I saw it and Freddy complained that his housekeeper wouldn't let him get rid of it because it was the only ornament in the whole house!' Molly's rueful smile of recollection slid away again. It had been over a fortnight since she had come home and that very same day she had returned Donald's ring. He had accepted her decision without questioning it but she had seen his concern when he'd recognised the desolation she was struggling to hide.

A slightly stout man with greying hair and warm brown eyes, Donald settled himself down on the sofa in her tiny lounge and regarded her consideringly. 'I really don't like blundering in where I know I'm not wanted—'

'Then don't!' Molly reddened and pushed an uneasy hand through her hair. 'I'm sorry, I'm not in the best of moods. My brother and his wife are living a nightmare right now and I feel so *helpless*!'

'But that's not the only reason you're feeling like this.' With instinctive tact, Donald averted his attention from her strained face. 'I have no idea what passed between you and Sholto but obviously the encounter caused you a lot of distress.'

Molly studied him with growing discomfiture. Donald looked so mild and unassuming that people were invariably surprised by the forthright character and plain speech which were as much a part of him as his caring nature. He was immensely popular with his parishioners. Indeed, since her stepfather's retirement and Donald's subsequent appointment as rector, the congregation had increased in strength. 'Donald—'

'And I know you won't be offended when I admit that after careful reflection I'm grateful you had the good sense to decide that we wouldn't suit. I would still very much like to have a wife to come home to at night...I rattle like a pea round the vicarage and I am lonely,' he admitted without sentimentality. 'But you *are* too young to settle for that sort of marriage. I'm afraid it was wishful thinking on my part but please don't let that proposal of mine make you feel uncomfortable with me now.'

Her eyes stung. His continuing friendship and understanding made her swallow hard and finally nod.

'So I hope I may still speak as a friend,' Donald continued wryly. 'Molly...for your own sake, start living in
the present and try to forget that Sholto ever existed. It's
the only way and I do *know* what I'm talking about.'

Both the reminder and the blunt advice made Molly
bite painfully at her lower lip. The woman Donald had
loved had returned his feelings but had shrunk from the
prospect of becoming a clergyman's wife. The relationship had trailed on unhappily for months before Donald
had finally gathered the strength to cut his losses and
end it.

'I'm not still in love with Sholto, Donald.' Molly
lifted her chin with fierce pride. 'In fact I dislike and
despise him!'

'Yet even now you change into a different person
when you've been with him,' Donald sighed. 'He winds
you up like a battery toy and then he leaves you flailing
around like a lost soul.'

Molly shivered as if an icy hand had trailed down her
spine. 'That's not a very comforting analogy.'

'But it's a true one. Don't forget that I was a spectator
to the after-effects of the first time around. I've seen you
like this before...one day you loved him, the next you
seemed to hate him with equal passion.'

Molly paled, her fingers curling on the chair-arm. She
had no desire to recall those dark days following an even
darker one four years ago, when the agony of betrayal
and humiliation had almost ripped her apart.

'Sadly nobody gave you impartial advice to begin
with,' Donald said regretfully. 'People whom you trusted
and who should've known better encouraged you to take
a hostile, embittered stance for various reasons of their
own. Your stepfather disliked Sholto and was delighted

to stand in judgement. Your mother backed up your step-father. And that girl, Jenna, your so-called best friend…' Donald pursed his lips expressively and continued, 'Jenna was bitterly envious of you from the day you met Sholto and was scarcely an unprejudiced bystander.'

Molly had stiffened defensively. 'I knew exactly what I was doing, Donald. Other people's opinions didn't influence me.'

'Well…I've said enough for now and I do have another call to make this evening.' Donald stood up unhurriedly. 'But has it ever occurred to you that *had* you allowed Sholto the chance to tell you his side of the story then the whole miserable affair would have been considerably less acrimonious?'

With a slight squirming sensation, Molly recalled Donald's unwelcome advice. He had urged her to seek such a meeting with Sholto but Molly had been deeply offended by a suggestion which had seemed to take no account of the fact that *she* was the injured party. It was only as she had got to know Donald better that she had learnt he could be a sincere and worthwhile friend.

She saw him out to his car. Donald was now talking cheerfully about his upcoming six-week vacation to visit relatives in New Zealand. He had been saving up for a long time to make the trip and was very much looking forward to it.

As Molly got ready for bed, she realised that Donald had made not one single reference to her brother Nigel's plight. Yet his sympathy had been pronounced…until she'd told him what Sholto had told her at Freddy's house. Perhaps Donald now thought that foolish Nigel was receiving his just deserts for playing Russian roulette with Sholto's money. But Molly's heart still ached for Nigel and his family.

Nigel didn't have a dishonest bone in his body and

he had all but cringed when she had confronted him with
Sholto's accusation of fraud. Yes, Sholto's bankers had
taken a similar stance, her brother had finally admitted,
but he had sworn that he had had no intent to defraud
anyone and had not even realised that the money was
not entirely his to do with as he wished. But then he had
not even studied the loan agreement, an admission which
had made Molly, who was a legal secretary, grind her
teeth in exasperation.

The next morning Molly felt even more exhausted
than she had the day before. She drove the five miles to
the small market town where she worked in a solicitor's
office and climbed the stairs with a heavy heart. Her
boss, Mr Woods, who had little patience with mistakes,
greeted her with a long legal brief which needed retyping
because she had misspelt the name of the client concerned.

Shortly before one o'clock she heard steps on the
stairs and glanced up with a frown, hoping it wasn't a
client because Mr Woods didn't like her to take her
lunch break while he still had someone in his office. On
the other hand, regardless of how late she might leave,
he would still expect her back at her desk by two.

The opaque glass door swung back, framing Sholto
on the threshold. In shock, Molly's heart leapt up into
her throat, something akin to raw panic assailing her. He
looked devastatingly handsome in a superbly cut dove-
grey suit that smoothly outlined his broad shoulders, narrow hips and long, powerful legs. His thick black hair
was brushed back off his brow, sleek stockbroker style,
the gleam of a white silk shirt accentuating the exotic
gold of his skin. Everything she had told herself she
wouldn't, couldn't, *mustn't* ever feel again hit her in
a tidal wave.

CHAPTER FOUR

RIVETING dark eyes rested on her, whipping down to the left hand bare of rings which Molly had braced on the edge of her desk. A wolfish smile drove the impassivity from Sholto's dark and vibrant features. 'Are you free for lunch?'

'L-lunch?' Molly stammered incredulously, the tip of her tongue stealing out to moisten her dry lips as she struggled to suppress the most terrifying surge of soaring excitement.

'What a drab and depressing working environment.' Sholto scanned the small, shabby reception area with its line of battered filing cabinets and the single narrow window which overlooked the roof of a neighbouring building. 'My employees would riot if I asked them to function in surroundings like these. I imagine you're overworked and underpaid too. You probably think it's better for your character.'

Still paralysed, Molly continued to stare at him, heart thundering, mouth dry as a bone. 'How on earth did you find out where I worked?'

'Freddy told me.' Sholto gave her a glinting look that was utterly unreadable. 'He had a habit of dropping little titbits unasked and I have a good memory.'

Molly flushed uneasily, wondering just how many 'little titbits' Freddy had passed on before her desultory correspondence with him had finally trailed to a halt. 'What are you doing here?'

'I've already covered that angle,' Sholto reminded her gently.

But why on earth would he ask her to join him for lunch? Her fine brows pleated as she stood up, fighting her own drowning, desperate self-consciousness with all her might. 'Was there something you—?'

'Did Donald take it badly?'

Registering the fact that he had noticed the missing engagement ring, Molly flung her head back, anger stirring. 'That's none of your business!'

'Together we made it my business,' Sholto countered softly. 'I don't make a habit of seducing women who have made promises to other men.'

Colour drenched her cheekbones. 'Donald and I had a sensible talk and simply decided that we wouldn't be suited,' she said with taut discomfiture.

An air of grim amusement softened the bold lines of his strong, dark face. 'I gather you didn't tell him how very lacking in sense you had been with me.'

Molly quivered, outraged that he could make that point to her face. 'I—'

'I'm not gloating, *cara*. But I do value candour,' Sholto told her drily. 'And once you did too. Yet you slapped me in the face and told me that you didn't want me when I know very well that you do.'

Completely disconcerted by that outspoken assurance, Molly was transfixed to the spot. Her rebellious memory chose that same moment to flash the image of that beautiful bronzed body of his against white linen sheets and the wild, exquisite torment of a lovemaking that had driven her out of her mind with excitement. Stunned by the intensity of that sexual imagery, she gazed blindly into shimmering golden eyes as compelling as the heart of a fire on an icy day, her legs trembling, her breasts rising and falling with the jerky rapidity of her breathing.

And then she remembered the aftermath, the *game* that he had taken to its merciless, cruelly humiliating conclusion, and the heat inside her was chilled by sudden instinctive fear. She turned her head away, breaking free of her overwhelming need to look at him with a sick sense of self-loathing.

'I have nothing more to say on that subject,' she informed him woodenly.

'*Dio*...there's not a lot you *can* say when you're lying through your teeth.'

Involuntarily Molly flinched and hated him. Dislike and despise, she had told Donald. And that had not been a lie. She had the susceptibility of a drug addict where Sholto was concerned but he had made her face the full destructive extent of her own weakness and she wore that experience now like a protective suit of armour. However, if there was the remotest chance that Sholto was here to discuss her brother's situation, she could scarcely afford to speak her mind. She spun back to him, heart-shaped face pale and tense, green eyes anxiously assessing.

'You mentioned lunch. Yet at this very moment your representatives are in the act of repossessing my brother's home and business.' Molly spelt out the unnecessary reminder uncomfortably. 'If you're here because you're willing to discuss Nigel's problems....'

A sardonic ebony brow had climbed, his spectacular bone structure clenching hard. 'I'm not...and I don't respond well to blackmail.'

'Blackmail?' Molly vented a shaken little laugh at the charge even as stark resentment and disappointment flooded her. 'And what could I possibly blackmail *you* with? Let me tell you something, Sholto...if it wasn't for the fact that Nigel is in a deep, dark hole I wouldn't even be speaking to you...indeed, I would already have shown you the door!'

Dense black lashes had swept low on his stunning dark eyes. 'Is that a fact?'

'Yes, that is a fact,' Molly confirmed in a shaking undertone as her temper rose in response to his unflinching cool. 'You have the legal right to do what you're doing to Nigel but don't expect me to like or respect you for it! Right now, on my own account, I would cross the street to avoid you! Dear heaven, don't you have any sense of decency? Your presence here now is an insult and an abuse of your power!'

'I don't believe I've ever been guilty of an abuse of power...or are you now saying that you slept with me in the hope that I might change my mind about your brother?' Sholto was oddly pale beneath his dark skin, slashing cheekbones rigid, eyes now a flash of burning, searing gold between his lashes.

The atmosphere simmered like a boiling cauldron.

Molly stilled in shock that he could even think her capable of using her body like a bargaining counter. Very pale, she lifted her head high and cleared her throat hoarsely. 'No, Sholto. That was a moment of madness...let that be my excuse,' she breathed, not quite evenly. 'No pressure and no price would *ever* be sufficient to persuade me to share a bed with you! I wouldn't behave like a tramp even for my brother's benefit!'

'"A moment of madness,"' Sholto repeated very softly, rolling the syllables darkly together as the glitter of his icy gaze raked her hotly flushed and angry face. 'You are quite, quite sure that it was nothing else?'

Molly slung him a look of defensive scorn. 'It was an accident, a mistake. What else did you think it might have been?'

Sholto surveyed her with chilling intensity. 'You may yet find out, *cara*.'

Molly snatched in a steadying breath, her legs quivering like cotton-wool sticks beneath her. 'I don't know what you're talking about but before you leave you are going to listen to what I have to say about Nigel. You gave a huge sum of money to a boy of twenty-three who left school at sixteen without a single exam pass to his name. He had no business experience, no training, no guidance and no supervision—'

'Per l'amor di Dio—'

'Nigel can't even balance a bank statement, Sholto,' she breathed in fiercely determined continuance, shot through with guilt for making that point and jerking her head hastily away before he could see the glimmer of tears in her eyes. 'But he knows just about everything there is to know about the horticultural end of the business and he is quite incapable of deliberately committing fraud. I blame *you* for the mess that he's in now! It was sheer insanity to give Nigel that money and then leave him alone to sink or swim!'

'Miss Bannister?' Molly whirled round in dismay to see Mr Woods standing on the threshold of his office. 'What is going on here?' he demanded with frowning incredulity.

His jawline hard as iron, Sholto released his breath in a slow, measured hiss. After shooting Molly a disturbingly intent look, he switched his attention smoothly to her boss. 'My apologies if we disturbed you,' he drawled, and then he swung fluidly on his heel and strode out the door without another word.

Molly dropped back down into her seat as if someone had suddenly kicked her feet out from under her. She was trembling, both shocked and proud that she had finally got to state her own opinion. Her employer hovered for a split second, glimpsed the tears sparkling on her cheeks and then headed for his raincoat like a homing pigeon. As his feet clattered in haste down the stairs, a ragged laugh fell from her lips. There she had been, tautly awaiting an outraged lecture, but poor Mr Woods couldn't escape fast enough from the threat of a crying secretary.

In the tiny cloakroom she splashed her face with cold water and with the greatest difficulty pulled herself together again. How *could* Sholto have come here in the midst of the nightmare her family were being forced to live and without a flicker of embarrassment invite her out to lunch? Didn't he have any sensibility at all? Had that same desire for revenge brought him here? Had he wanted the satisfaction of confirming that her engagement had been broken? No doubt he would laugh if he ever found out that Donald didn't even know that for the space of a day she had actually worn his ring and planned to marry him.

But what on earth had Sholto meant when he had asked her if it had only been a moment of madness on her part when they had made love? How had he expected her to respond?

After work she drove over to Nigel and Lena's house. Pillars worthy of a Texan mansion embellished the entire frontage and a big extension had been added to the rear. Not a trace of the old farmhouse's former damp, dry rot and dilapidation remained. Her eldest niece, Sally, was sitting forlornly on the back step of the conservatory, her little face tear-stained and pale.

Molly crouched down beside the eight-year-old with anxious eyes. 'What's wrong?'

'Mum says I'll have to go to a new school...and I won't have any friends there,' Sally said tremulously. 'I don't want to have to go to a new school. I like the one I'm at.'

Molly walked into the messy kitchen which had until recently been her sister-in-law's pride and joy. These days Lena was letting the house go in much the same way that she was letting herself go. A small, slight woman with untidy fair hair, she gave Molly a dull look from swollen blue eyes, her depression palpable.

'Sally's talking about changing schools.'

'We can't find anywhere we can afford to rent around here,' Lena muttered tightly. 'And the waiting list for council housing is a mile long. She'll have to go to another school. We did ask your stepfather if he could put us up for a while but he started laying into Nigel and there was a huge row and that was the end of that.'

They must've been desperate to even consider approaching her stepfather for help, Molly thought grimly. George Gilpin had remarried two years after her mother's death and was now enjoying his retirement in his present wife's comfortable bungalow some miles outside the village—but he had never invited his stepchildren to visit him there.

'Where's Nigel?' Molly asked.

'I don't know. He went over to the garden centre as usual first thing this morning and this man was waiting for him. The man asked for the keys and said *he* was in charge now and that Nigel could go home again,' Lena recited, her voice thickening with sudden tears. 'So it's finally started. They've put a manager in to run the business until they can sell it…and next month it will be the house. Nigel was in an awful state…he just took off in my car and he hasn't come back and I don't know where to turn because I n-never really thought it would come to this!'

Molly curved an arm round the smaller woman's quivering shoulders and pressed her down into a chair.

Sally's sister, Fiona, wandered in, trailing a torn carrier bag stuffed with soft toys in her wake. 'I'm packing,' she announced with all the importance of a four-year-old seeking praise for being helpful.

Lena took one look at her younger daughter's innocent face and went off into gasping, shuddering sobs of misery, burying her face in her arms over the table. In response, Fiona burst into frightened tears and the toddler in the play-pen behind the door set up a piercing howl in sympathy.

Molly concentrated on the children, lifting her nephew, Robin, out of the play-pen and wafting him and Fiona through to the lounge where their toys were. But in all her life she could never recall feeling so utterly useless. She lived in a tiny rented flat with one bedroom and could offer no assistance on the accommodation front.

Nigel and Lena had got married in their teens. Molly's grandfather had allowed them to live with him and until his death he had employed Nigel at a poverty-line wage in his market gardening business.

Sholto had never seen how Nigel and Lena had lived then. Lena had shrunk from the prospect of entertaining Sholto in their damp, run-down home. So they had caught the train to London and met Sholto in his breathtaking Georgian town house instead. Molly still remembered the two of them sitting in that vast drawing room in their very best clothes, hugely intimidated both by Sholto and their surroundings and then shellshocked when Sholto had carelessly offered them the finance to make Nigel's dreams come true.

Having been desperately short of money all their married life, they had then been as wildly extravagant and foolish as a pair of reckless children, and now they were paying the price.

Molly stayed until her brother came home at eight. By then she had persuaded Lena to go for a nap and had fed and put the children to bed. Nigel had a blank look in his bloodshot eyes when he came into the lounge and found her there. He looked exhausted, face drawn, shoulders slumped in defeat.

'I suppose Lena told you about the new manager over at the garden centre?' he mumbled heavily. 'Well, as our old stepdad put it, once a loser always a loser. Academic failure and now failed businessman.'

Driving back to her flat a few minutes later, Molly was still recoiling from her stepfather's cruelty. Nothing like kicking Nigel when he was already down. The phone was ringing as she came through the front door. Wearily thrusting the door shut behind her, she reached for the receiver.

'It's Sholto, Molly.'

The silence crackled on the line. She couldn't think of a single thing to say.

'I have a business proposition to put to you and, yes, it does concern your brother,' Sholto outlined softly. 'I'll see you in my office to discuss it at two o'clock tomorrow afternoon.'

Molly gulped. She was in a daze, unable to think straight. 'But I'm working... No, it'll be OK...I'll *be* there!' she stressed, terrified the offer might be withdrawn.

'Shall I send a car to pick you up?' Sholto enquired pleasantly. 'You never did like driving in city traffic.'

'No...thank you, I'll catch the train.'

Breathless and stunned, Molly replaced the receiver and then almost reached for it again to call Nigel. But she snatched her hand back from temptation. No, she'd better not say anything until she had seen Sholto. Had something she said this afternoon struck a compassionate chord with him? She shook her head numbly, still reeling with shock.

Funnily enough, she would have thought that her having shouted at Sholto would have put him in an absolute freezing rage because he was considerably less accustomed to censure than other, more ordinary mortals. But if she hadn't shouted he would never have listened...

Cristaldi Investments occupied a strikingly contemporary building in the City. As Molly took her seat in the breathtakingly elegant waiting area on the executive floor, she found the soaring stainless-steel pillars and preponderance of tinted glass coldly intimidating. But it hadn't always been like that. She could remember once charging out of the lift, cheerfully brushing aside the receptionist's objections to announce her intention of surprising Sholto, bouncily secure in the knowledge that he had asked her to marry him the night before.

Then Pandora had been in his office, draped elegantly across a designer couch and looking maddeningly at home there.

'I believe congratulations are in order,' she had said laconically. 'Sholto's in a meeting. Is he expecting you?'

'Well, no, but I...I thought we could have lunch.'

'We're flying to Paris in a couple of hours. I'm afraid you've chosen a bad day to drop in,' Pandora had drawled with pseudo-sympathy.

At that point, that had been the longest conversation she had ever had with Sholto's cousin. Pandora's blue eyes had been as cold as icicles. Only when they had got engaged had Pandora deigned to take notice of her and it had not been the kind of notice Molly found comfortable. As the weeks had passed, she had begun to resent and dislike the woman who seemed to be seamlessly entwined with almost every part of Sholto's life.

Sholto and Pandora had had the same friends, the same lifestyle, the same wealth, the same tastes. Pandora had walked in and out of Sholto's house as if she owned it, played hostess whenever he entertained, borrowed his shirts and sweaters and cracked clever jokes which had made Sholto laugh while Molly was still waiting on the punchline. Molly had hovered like a pretender to the throne, outmatched in looks, sparkle and sophistication, but Sholto hadn't appeared to notice that there was a problem.

More and more she had found herself wondering exactly *why* Sholto should have asked her to marry him. He hadn't mentioned love. He had pulled her close and said with the utmost cool and casualness, 'Let's get married.'

And she had been stunned, her wildest dreams fulfilled without warning. She had only been seeing him for two months and every time she had gone out with him she had had to fight her way past her stepfather's grimly humiliating forecast that she was being led up the garden path by a rich and immoral playboy. Sholto's reputation with women had gone before him and the evening that Sholto had made the very great error of actually correcting the Reverend Mr Gilpin on an obscure point of theology her stepfather's rigid disapproval had blazed into outright loathing.

Their engagement had shocked everyone. Sholto's friends hadn't even bothered to hide the fact. Molly had reacted by trying to change herself into a more socially acceptable person. She had dieted with fervour, cut and tinted her hair first chestnut then red and finally blonde, and had run up a huge overdraft buying horribly expensive and more daring clothes.

She had been jealous of Pandora, had struggled not to be, had not to the bitter end realised that Pandora's relationship with Sholto was anything other than it appeared to be. The two of them had been so frighteningly, cruelly clever. After all, right up until the wedding, Sholto's cousin had feverishly dated and ditched one man after another, rarely making an appearance without some besotted male by her side.

'Miss Bannister?'

Abruptly snatched out of the past, Molly glanced up uncertainly to find the receptionist trying to attract her attention.

'Mr Cristaldi is ready to see you now. His office is at the foot of the corridor.'

Molly nodded as if she were a first-time visitor. She was grateful not to be recognised. But then who would remember her now, a one-day wonder of a bride, left to sink back into merciful obscurity as soon as some other unfortunate had grabbed the headlines? She smoothed down the pleated skirt of her green wool suit. It was the one she wore to church and was about as exciting as cold porridge. But Sholto hadn't invited her here to look at her, had he?

She opened one side of the impressive carved double doors jerkily and stepped onto the soft deep carpet beyond with a heart thumping like a mechanical hammer out of control.

'Full marks for punctuality.' Sholto straightened from his easy lounging stance against his gleaming glass desk and strode forward with effortless grace. 'Would you like to sit down?'

With muffled thanks that went awry on her lips, she sat down on the very edge of a leather chair that had a most peculiar shape. Through the tinted windows she might have seen a panoramic view of the city but Sholto occupied her entire attention. He was smiling, which ought to have been encouraging but somehow something in the quality of that smile struck her as rather threatening.

He rested back against his desk again, fluid as a cat and at first glance looking staggeringly conservative in a navy pinstriped suit. But a closer perusal revealed the distinctive hallmarks of smooth Italian designer style accentuated by an exotic gold tie that in some lights probably reflected his eyes, Molly found herself thinking abstractedly. She reddened with fierce guilt and looked at the carpet instead.

'I really appreciated your call last night,' she murmured tautly, hoping to heaven she didn't sound as crawly and servile to him as she did to herself.

'Perhaps you had better hear what I have to say first.'

Molly nodded, forcing her gaze slowly up again, taking in polished, hand-stitched shoes, the perfect drape of his trousers on his long, powerful legs, the breadth of his chest behind that beautifully cut double-breasted jacket, the strong angle of his faintly blue-shadowed jaw…the perfectly curved lips breaking into a blindingly brilliant and amused smile.

'Yes, it has been a long time since you saw me yesterday,' Sholto commented lazily.

He sounded like a big cat purring after a kill. Alarm bells rang like klaxons in Molly's head. He had sounded like that, all sexy and silkily reassuring, in Freddy's feather bed and look what had happened to her then!

Unwarily she tipped her head back and met the dark, impenetrable eyes fixed on her. Her colour fluctuated wildly as she waited in that pin-dropping silence for him to speak.

'Nigel isn't on my conscience, Molly,' he stated quietly. 'I feel I should make that point first. I gave him a golden opportunity and he blew it. I knew he was no business whizkid but my bankers did recommend an excellent accountant. Your brother stopped using his services as soon as the garden centre was built, probably because the accountant was already telling him things he didn't want to hear.'

Molly said nothing. There was nothing she could say. The internal workings of her brother's business were a closed book to her.

'And when Nigel started getting into trouble my bankers wrote to him. At that stage he might still have been pulled back from the edge of his financial abyss. But he ignored their letters. When they visited the garden centre, he told his staff to say he was out. When they went to the house, your sister-in-law refused to open the door.'

Molly licked her dry lips. 'Your bankers were very menacing.'

'*Dio*…what would you expect when they were getting the runaround like that?' Sholto shot at her in complete exasperation.

Not liking the dangerous turn the conversation had taken, not wishing Sholto to dwell too long on her brother's undeniable deficiencies, Molly conceded awkwardly, 'Nigel behaved very foolishly.'

'Nigel's a total idiot!' Sholto spread expressive brown hands. 'And believe me, *cara*, it goes against the grain to even consider giving him another chance to prove himself.'

'He's learnt his lesson. He *really* has,' Molly emphasised pleadingly. 'He would do whatever you wanted him to do to sort things out.'

'And what about you?'

Molly blinked. 'But I don't have anything to do with the garden centre.'

Brilliant dark eyes swept over her frowning face and lingered. 'I am not talking about the business. You said that no pressure and no price would persuade you to share my bed. I'm calling your bluff,' Sholto delivered silkily. 'If you move into my house and live with me, I will settle your brother's debts, allow him to remain in his home and ensure that he doesn't get himself into a similar mess a second time.'

For a count of ten paralysed seconds, Molly gaped at him with startled green eyes and parted lips. 'You're not serious,' she framed when she could finally unpeel her tongue from the roof of her mouth.

'I want you...and you want your brother off the hook. A fair exchange or an abuse of my power?' Sholto mused with galling cool. 'I shall leave you to decide which.'

Molly tried and failed to swallow, brows pleating as she squirmed uneasily on her seat. 'You are joking, aren't you?'

'Do I look like I'm joking?'

She noted with disbelief that he had a perfectly straight face.

'But why would you want me to live with you?' Molly enquired helplessly.

'All the usual male reasons,' Sholto supplied with gentle, slightly apologetic emphasis. 'I wasn't planning to stash you in a guest room as a hostage to Nigel's good behaviour in the future. I would expect you to sleep in my bed with me, wear the clothes that I buy, appear at social occasions by my side and be available to travel with me whenever I ask.'

Molly's heart thudded with preternatural slowness in her eardrums. Every word he said echoed twice over inside her head. He had spelt out his expectations with clarity. But she could no more see herself featuring in such an existence than she could see herself taking flight without wings. 'I want you', he had said, in much the same casual manner as he might have voiced the selection of a meal from a menu.

He couldn't possibly want her so much that he was prepared to bribe her to get back into bed with him. Unless his sole motivation was the sheer senseless and stubborn perversity of a macho male hopelessly ill equipped to deal with any form of female rejection! After all, she had slapped his face and walked out of the late Freddy's house and refused to engage in any remotely personal dialogue when he'd come to the office where she worked. Sholto was not accustomed to that kind of treatment.

'You're actually suggesting that I become your mistress?' she murmured, her incredulity unconcealed.

'That's a very old-fashioned and emotive label, Molly,' Sholto responded in a tone of reproof. 'Live-in relationships are very common these days.'

'You're talking about couples who freely *choose* to live together!'

'You have a choice too.'

'And those same couples would naturally have feelings for each other!' Molly pointed out rawly.

'Whereas I'm proposing an exclusively physical affair. You see, I was deeply unimpressed by the staying power of your *feelings* when we married,' Sholto countered with derisive bite. 'I was infinitely more impressed by your passionate response in bed two weeks ago...'

A little shudder of repulsion ran through Molly, her mortification rising by the minute. 'I think you brought me here purely to humiliate me. What gave you the idea that I might be prepared to barter my body like some sort of commodity in exchange for my family's security?'

'You gave me the idea yesterday.'

'I...*did*?' she gasped.

'Would you like me to have some coffee brought in while you mull over the dangerous risk of descending into a life of sleazy decadence after a mere few months in my bed?'

Flashes of hot colour stained Molly's cheekbones. She didn't appreciate his drawling mockery and, determined to walk out, she flew upright in one swift and angry movement. Simultaneously a wave of dizziness engulfed her and she swayed, darkness flashing across her vision as the room spun and her head pounded. A pair of strong hands immediately steadied her, curving round her shoulders and pressing her firmly back down onto the seat.

'Are you all right?'

Dizzily she focused on Sholto, crouched down in front of her, dark eyes raking her bemused face with frowning intensity. 'I thought you were going to faint.'

'I've never fainted in my life.'

Looking surprisingly pale and tense, Sholto very slowly slid upright again. 'I'll bring you a glass of water.'

'I must've stood up too fast. I skipped lunch.' And only had coffee for breakfast, she completed inwardly. No doubt all the stress and tension had reacted badly on her empty stomach and made her light-headed.

A moisture-beaded glass bumped against her fingers. He must have moved with the speed of light. She sipped the water, feeling distinctly foolish at having been deprived of her haughty exit.

'How are you feeling now?'

'Perfectly fine,' Molly said stiffly. 'You know I was about to leave?'

'That's your decision.' Sholto strolled over to the tall windows, the sunlight gleaming over his arrogant dark head to accentuate his spectacular cheekbones and the ruthless cast of his mouth. He gazed back at her steadily, glittering eyes gilded to gold. 'But bear in mind that I won't repeat this offer.'

'You should never have made it. I don't know where you got the nerve to even *think* that I would consider such an arrangement!' Molly told him with sudden fire.

'I don't suffer from nerves, Molly. When I want something I go after it and I'll do whatever it takes to get it. You were the one who brought the commercial aspect into this—'

'*I* was?' she interrupted incredulously.

'You're only here now because of your brother.'

Shoulders and spine rigid, Molly rose to her feet. 'I'm glad you appreciate that fact.'

'I do admire your spirit. Obviously you feel more than equal to the task of supporting Nigel and Lena through their coming ordeal,' Sholto murmured smoothly as she turned on her heel. 'I would say that both of them are rather weak reeds in the face of adversity. And the apparent menace of my bankers will be as nothing next to the infinitely more aggressive tactics likely to be employed by Nigel's *other* creditors.'

Involuntarily Molly's feet faltered on their passage to the door. 'What are you trying to say?'

'That the instant my people put the garden centre on the market Nigel's other creditors will take fright and descend like a hoard of locusts. Then the courts and the bailiffs will become involved.'

Molly had a mental image of Fiona's soft toys being snatched from her by some big, brawny, aggressive man. Her stomach heaved. Bailiffs. The threatening, final response to unsettled debts. She knew nothing about bailiffs but somehow the very mention of them struck cold horror into her bones.

As she slowly turned back to look at Sholto, she watched his slow smile build and wild, bitter anger flooded her. She felt like a puppet having its strings pulled. 'You can't possibly want a woman who hates your guts!'

'Hate me the way you hated me at Freddy's house and I have this extraordinary feeling that I will thrive,' Sholto asserted with immense cool.

CHAPTER FIVE

'I DON'T know why I'm still here,' Molly gritted.

But the trouble was that she knew all too well and that bitter awareness was of no comfort. Sholto had the power to end Nigel and Lena's nightmare. The power to work a miracle and restore an entire family to happy and secure normality. But he also had the power to make her sit back down again in his wretched fancy office when she didn't want to and feel trapped. And that acknowledgement was by far the most frightening.

Sholto was on the phone, his bold, bronzed profile aloof, but his beautifully shaped hands moved in eloquent shifts to sketch vivid word pictures as he talked. Molly studied him with compulsive intensity. If she lived to be a hundred she would never understand Sholto. When they'd been engaged, he had treated her as if she had a defensive barrier round her body, yet four years on, when she had least expected such a move, he had pounced without conscience and shattered her with the apparent force of his desire.

But that had just been sex and where Sholto was concerned Molly held the cynical belief that he was very much a male to whom sex was no big deal. Few women were out of his reach and even fewer said no to him. From adolescence, Sholto had been the frequently bored target of female craving, pursuit and encouragement. She had watched him employ that cool detachment of his to freeze out unwelcome advances. So many beautiful, *willing* women—what could he possibly see in her?

'Revenge,' Molly condemned with driven abruptness. 'Is that what this is all about?'

Sholto set down the phone.

'Do you get a sick thrill out of forcing me to agree to something that goes against every principle I have?' she demanded starkly.

'Will you get one when I rehabilitate your immature, irresponsible and thoroughly unreliable brother? *That* goes against every principle *I* have. And if you feel you're being forced you should leave now,' Sholto advised. 'You made this strictly business, Molly. Emotional appeals are way out of line.'

Molly threw her head back in a jerky movement, green eyes feverishly bright. 'And where does Pandora come into this arrangement?'

Sholto stilled but his stunning dark eyes remained utterly level. 'She doesn't. Any other questions?'

Molly looked through him, shutting him out while she worked at keeping her face carefully blank. The question had been irresistible. She had had to ask even though asking had been like twisting a knife inside an open wound. A light knock sounded on the door, granting her a badly needed breathing space in which to recover.

Sholto set a tray down on the low table next to her. Molly gaped at it. The serving of tea and buttered toast struck her as quite hysterically inappropriate in the circumstances.

'I thought you should eat something.'

'I feel more like alcohol than tea,' she confided rather raggedly.

'I keep nothing like that in the office,' Sholto asserted.

Briefly, Molly focused on the carved oriental drinks cabinet with a confused frown and then she poured herself a cup of tea because of course she hadn't been serious about the alcohol. Sholto extended the plate of toast. 'No, thanks.'

'Be sensible,' Sholto told her drily.

Molly took a piece of toast, wondering why he was so ridiculously keen to see her eat, but she was under too much strain to make an issue of it.

Silence fell while she ate.

'I don't want you to go home tonight.'

Molly almost choked on her last piece of toast, coughed and then swallowed with difficulty. 'Are you crazy?'

A winged ebony brow rose. 'I'll make arrangements for a temp to take over your job for a month at my expense. That'll give your employer time to find a replacement—'

'I couldn't leave Mr Woods in the lurch like that. I *have* to work a month's notice!' Molly protested in pure panic.

'Any experienced legal secretary could do your work.'

'Sholto—'

'If you move in today, I'll drive down and see Nigel tomorrow morning. The longer it takes you to move in, the longer he will wait to have his mind set at rest.' Sholto spelt out that cruel reality without an ounce of discomfiture. 'We don't have a deal until you are physically in residence.'

Molly paled, thinking of the desperate state her brother had been in the night before, reluctantly recalling how disturbed she had been that Nigel had left Lena alone all day to worry about his whereabouts. 'But I—'

'I'll have professional packers into your apartment by Monday at the latest.'

Feeling as though he was taking over her whole life, Molly bridled. 'No...that's quite unnecessary.'

'Allow me to decide what's necessary.' Sholto drew

her up out of her seat and lifted a seemingly idle hand to trace the stiff compression of her lips with a reproving fingertip.

Molly shivered and tossed her head back out of reach, skittish as a racehorse at the starting line. He closed his hands round her narrow wrists and drew her inexorably closer. 'Let go of me,' she told him tightly.

Brilliant dark eyes inspected her mutinous face. 'Unwilling sacrifices don't attract me, *cara*.'

'What did you expect?'

'I don't know.' A self-mocking smile tugged unexpectedly at the corners of his wide, sensual mouth. 'I have to confess that I didn't think that far ahead.'

Mere inches separated them and yet nothing short of physical force could have made Molly retreat from the proximity of that lean, powerful body of his. The very scent of him...clean, warm and male...sentenced her to paralysed stillness. As she stared up at him, dry throat convulsing, heart banging like crazy against her ribs, he closed his arms round her. Her eyes flew wide, a soft sound of shock escaping her as the rigid thrust of his arousal pressed against her belly. A surge of liquid heat flared between her thighs and he slid his hands down to her hips, hitching her skirt to lift her up against him and claim her mouth in a shatteringly sexual kiss.

He kissed with the same breathtaking eroticism with which he made love. The world spun violently as he let his tongue delve in a sinuous flick between her lips and tease the sensitive interior within. An anguished moan of response was dredged from low in her throat. Her bones turned to water, her flesh to yielding pliancy as she wrapped her arms round his neck. He slid her down to the carpet again but kept her imprisoned with one powerful hand splayed across her spine and then he lifted his dark head.

His eyes blazed like golden arrows in his lean, hard-boned face. '*Dio*...you looked as wholesome as Joan of Arc about to burn at the stake when you walked in here—'

'Sholto—'

He gazed down at her with sudden vibrant amusement. 'All temptingly packaged from throat to mid-calf in shapeless green tweed. Alas my memory is not so short, *cara*. I shall forever cherish the image of you sliding out of my T-shirt.'

At the same instant as he set her back from him, Molly's hands came up to push him away. The turbulence of her confused emotions was threatening to rip her apart. He had swept her up like a toy and kissed her breathless and she hadn't done a thing to prevent him. In the aftermath, she didn't even know how it had happened and that terrified her. He had smashed her self-control with effortless ease.

'Revenge has got nothing to do with this,' Sholto drawled very quietly. 'And I did not bring you here with any intent of humiliating you. The past doesn't come into this either. It's dead and gone but we're *not*. I've wanted you ever since that snowy night at Freddy's house...'

'And what you want you have to have,' Molly extended, her throat thickening. 'No matter what the cost.'

He swept up his mobile phone, scanning her with impenetrable eyes. 'Let's just say I don't mind paying for the privilege of your presence but I would have respected you a whole lot more if you had come of your own accord and without preconditions.'

Molly folded her arms, afraid he might notice that her hands were shaking. He turned her life upside down within the space of an hour and behaved as if that were normal. But then Sholto had no concept of upheaval because he had never experienced it. His wealth protected him from ninety-nine per cent of the inconveniences and crises that dogged other people's lives. He lifted a phone and for the right price he could have just about anything. And only then did Molly fully appreciate, with a sick sensation in her stomach, that he had lifted the phone and employed exactly the same technique with *her*...

Sholto straightened with an impatient frown. 'I'm afraid I'm tied up for the rest of the afternoon and I have a board meeting this evening. My driver will take you back to the house. Stop off at Harrods and buy whatever you need for the night,' he advised, withdrawing his wallet with a sardonic glance at her burning face. 'Please don't be squeamish about spending my money. After all, Nigel is going to cost me a small fortune...disasters are rarely cost-effective, so why quibble about a triviality?'

Her arms unfolded with an outraged jerk and her hands clenched into two admirable fists. For a split second, she wasn't even sure she could hold onto her temper. 'I'll never forgive you for doing this to me!'

Unaffected by the assurance, Sholto settled a huge wad of notes into her bag, hooked it back deftly over her shoulder and curved a calm hand round her slender spine to push her gently towards the door. 'Keep one fact in mind, Molly...Joan of Arc *burned*. As a role model for survival, she hasn't got a lot to offer.'

A uniformed chauffeur was already waiting for her out at Reception. They travelled down in the lift to the underground car park. Opening the passenger door of the limousine, he enquired, 'Are we to go straight back to the house, Miss Bannister?'

'No, my instructions are to stop off at Harrods on the way,' Molly responded in an undertone, almost choked with rage.

Sholto couldn't be doing this to her; he simply

couldn't be doing this to her! The Joan of Arc analogy returned to haunt her. Her teeth ground together. *She* was *allowing* him to do this to her, conniving in her own downfall because she did not have a hard enough heart to stand back and watch while her brother's family fell apart. She was extremely fond of her nephew and nieces. The children were already suffering and without Sholto's intervention Molly knew that there would be far, far worse to come.

Oh, sure, left to themselves, Nigel and Lena would eventually find somewhere else to live, but then the bitterness and the mutual recriminations would probably set in. How long, for instance, would it take Nigel to find a job? He had no qualifications in a job market where qualifications were essential. And only the very strongest marriage would survive poverty and unemployment on top of the loss of a dream home and business.

Nigel and Lena loved each other but Sholto...damn him to hell and back for his insight!...had been right on target when he'd said that neither party had impressed him as having much in the way of endurance. In all the months since his debts had started mounting, Nigel had done not one effective thing to help himself, and Lena, shorn of his support, had merely sunk deeper into depression and self-pity.

Molly made her purchases in Harrods in record time. She bought a change of underwear, a few toiletries, and if she dallied at all it was over her careful choice of night attire.

Sholto's butler, Ogden, had the front door of the town house open even before she alighted from the limousine. 'Good afternoon, Miss Bannister...may I say how very pleasant it is to see you again?'

Her face hot with discomfiture, Molly stiltedly refused

an offer of afternoon tea and followed in the wake of Ogden's majestic passage up the stairs. Her last meeting with the older man had taken place on her wedding night when she had been surprised in the act of trailing two suitcases down this selfsame staircase. Ogden had been aghast.

'Don't do this...*please* don't do this, madam!' he had exclaimed, shock and dismay at such a turn of events puncturing his usual poker-face formality.

'Did you try to stop Sholto leaving?' Molly had sobbed.

Ogden had looked distinctly uncomfortable because nobody, least of all a humble employee, would ever dare to try and stop Sholto doing anything. Molly had seen strong men quail when Sholto walked into a room. His brilliant manoeuvres in the world of high finance intimidated his own executives. And in his London home Sholto received unquestioning loyalty and devotion from a household staff whose senior members, by virtue of their long service, could only be described as family retainers.

'He was a horribly lonely and isolated child,' Freddy had once told her on one of his trips south after their engagement. 'His father was a workaholic, always flying off somewhere on business, and his mother, my niece, *well*...Olivia was a rather cold fish to say the least and she didn't believe in mollycoddling children. Thought it was good for Sholto to be toughened up, never showed him any affection, don't think she knew *how*. You see, she was brought up the same way.'

At the time, that information had affected Molly deeply and it had also bolstered her against the often daunting challenge of Sholto's detachment. He didn't like to show his feelings, she had told herself. Of course he *loved* her, he just wasn't comfortable talking about that sort of stuff. He simply preferred things low-key and unemotional. She had been so blind, so eager to make excuses for him, she reflected wretchedly.

Ogden cleared his throat.

Dredged from her painful ruminations, Molly registered the fact that he was waiting for her to precede him through the door now standing wide on the master bedroom suite. It was patently obvious that Sholto had already made it clear that this was where she would be spending her nights. Her face furiously flushed, she crossed the threshold, only slightly relieved to discover that the elegant sitting room had been redecorated and re-furnished.

'Mr Cristaldi thought you might wish to lie down before dinner,' Ogden said.

Suddenly Molly wanted to race downstairs and sprint round the block until she dropped dead from exhaustion. The door quietly closed on Ogden. What the hell was Sholto playing at? She wanted to tear her hair out and scream with frustration! She was beginning to feel terrifyingly like that battery toy Donald had mentioned, utterly powerless to make a move without Sholto's input and direction. Why was he doing this to her...*why*? She refused to accept that Sholto, with his iron self-discipline, could be seriously focusing on her as a tormenting sexual object of must-have desire. But then when had she *ever* known what went on inside Sholto's head? And once again time slipped back for her...

Relations between them had been strained before they'd even made it to the altar but Molly had staunchly blamed herself for that. She should have been blissfully happy during the four months that ran up to their wedding but instead she had become increasingly anxious and insecure. It had been far more difficult to fit into

Sholto's world than she had ever envisaged, particularly with Pandora around.

There had been severe strife in her home life as well. Sholto had refused to let her stepfather conduct the wedding ceremony. Bluntly averse to the concept of being married off by a man who loathed him, he had insisted on engaging another clergyman. Outraged at being passed over, Molly's stepfather had sarcastically suggested that Sholto take over *all* the wedding arrangements. Sholto had seized on the idea with alacrity and acted on it, choosing a London church, to be followed by a reception at his town house. Deep offence had been caused and from that point on the atmosphere in the vicarage had been poisonous.

During those months, Molly had thrown several emotional scenes which had driven Sholto into aloof retreat. She had been shaken by his arrogant refusal to compromise for the sake of peace and frankly frightened by his chilling silence if she pressed him too hard. Then he had taken off to the jungles of Indonesia for three solid weeks and before he had left he had totally devastated her by telling her that she was driving him clean up the wall with her immature demands and tantrums.

'So sort yourself out before I get back…or there won't be a wedding to worry about,' Sholto had completed grimly.

He had called a day later from the other side of the world and apologised, indeed had sworn he hadn't meant a word of it, but Molly had never quite recovered from that first alarming encounter with Sholto's cold anger and painfully cutting tongue. She had been so desperately in love with him and so terrified of losing him. From that day on, she had lived with the humiliating fear that Sholto just might suddenly decide not to marry her after all.

And when their wedding day had arrived she had been punch-drunk with relief once that ceremony was over. Indeed, she had been at the very height of happy over-excitement when she had noticed, during the closing stages of their reception, that Sholto was nowhere to be seen. She had naturally taken off in search of him, had heard his voice as she hurried down the corridor that led to his library on the first floor, had been smiling with complete serenity when she'd reached out to push wide the ajar door...

And then she had heard Pandora as she had never heard her before...and she had hesitated, her fingers freezing on the door handle. She had not opened that door wider, had not advertised her presence. Frankly she had been too shattered by sick disbelief to do anything but back away and then run before either of them could realise that they had been overheard.

Closing her aching eyes, Molly sank heavily down on a lemon brocade sofa and struggled to shut out the memory of that agonising moment of revelation. It took ferocious concentration to achieve such a feat of mental censorship. For months afterwards, she had been tortured by bad dreams, waking up in a cold sweat of fear to dazedly register the fact that she was not still trapped by appalled paralysis outside that same door, having her every illusion of happiness brutally torn from her.

'It's only because *she* can give you children...and I can't... You wouldn't have married her otherwise!' Pandora had been sobbing brokenly. 'Oh, God, I can't bear it—I can't *bear* to share you with her!'

'Nothing will change between us,' Sholto had sworn in a low, deep voice wrenched with more emotion than Molly had ever known he possessed. 'You will always have a place in my heart and I will always be here for you when you need me. I can promise you that.'

With a strangled moan of shivering remembrance, Molly thrust her damp and convulsing face into a feather cushion. They had talked like lovers forcibly separated by some impossibly cruel circumstance, Pandora sobbing as if her heart was breaking, Sholto sounding like a complete stranger to Molly in his intensely supportive tenderness.

That they should have a relationship which went far beyond the platonic front they had been so careful to maintain in public had been a devastating betrayal. She had not understood why the truth should ever have been concealed as if it were something to be ashamed of. All she had grasped that night was that Sholto had married her because she could give him children and Pandora could not, that while Molly might be his wife Pandora was the woman he loved. And it had seemed brutally obvious to Molly that neither of them had the slightest intention of allowing Sholto's marriage to interrupt their secret affair.

CHAPTER SIX

As a hand shook her shoulder, Molly shifted uncomfortably within the confinement of her rucked-up skirt, dimly wondering what she was doing lying down in all her clothes. Her lashes flickered and lifted with drowsy slowness. She looked straight into a pair of stunning, dark, deep-set eyes on a level with her own. It was like being run over by a truck without warning. Her body jerked and her heart thudded as she snatched in a startled gulp of oxygen.

'Were you waiting up for me?' Sholto treated her to a slashing smile of amusement and vaulted lithely upright. 'I'm impressed, really impressed, *cara*. I had envisaged several possible scenarios but this was not one of them.'

Molly hauled herself up on the sofa and hurriedly clawed her skirt down over her exposed thighs. The last thing she recalled was a manservant removing the tray on which she had opted to eat her evening meal. 'I wasn't waiting up for you,' she disclaimed with unnecessary force. 'I must've fallen asleep!'

'Better and better.' Sholto shrugged his broad shoulders fluidly out of his well-cut jacket and tossed the garment carelessly onto a nearby chair. 'I am obviously not about to hear a plea of complete exhaustion.'

Her face burning, Molly studied the antique carriage clock on the marble mantelpiece. 'It's *only* half past ten,' she pointed out frigidly, her restive fingers coiling round the hem of her skirt to pleat a slice of fabric nervously.

'I don't know why it is,' Sholto confided reflectively

as he jerked loose the knot on his gold silk tie and trailed it off with a lazy brown hand, 'but all afternoon and all evening I have had this desperate craving for an early night.'

Stiffening at that unvarnished statement of intent, Molly snatched in a ragged breath and tilted her chin. 'I don't want to go to bed with you,' she told him baldly. 'But if I have to I will.'

'Ah…' Sholto breathed with an air of grim satisfaction at evidently having his expectations finally and fully met. 'You're hoping to make me feel guilty but I'm afraid you're out of luck with that ploy. I've never bedded an unwilling woman in my life and I have no ambition to start with you. The prospect of ravishing a human sacrifice does not thrill me in the slightest…and if that is the best you can do I suggest that you remove yourself to the guest room next door and go home in the morning.'

Molly had gone from hot pink to pale. Never having met with the kind of ruthless negotiating tactics at which Sholto excelled, she was utterly disconcerted by his instantaneous rejection of the stance she had taken. 'That's quite a speech.'

'And it should have been an unnecessary one. I believe I spelt out the entire deal in terms a toddler could have understood this afternoon.'

Molly flushed. 'Stop talking about this like it's some sort of business deal!' she condemned, rising restively to her feet because nervous tension would no longer allow her to remain still.

'But that is *exactly* what it is.' Sholto's brilliant dark eyes ran consideringly over her stricken face and he shifted one shoulder in a fluid shrug. 'When I have to pay for the pleasure of having you here, what else would you call this arrangement? Although I believe I could muster several rather less savoury descriptions.'

Molly regarded him in stunned reproach. 'You offered *me* this arrangement!'

'But when did I say that I would respect you for agreeing to it?' Sholto countered with lethal effect as he strode into the connecting bedroom. 'And when you have the hypocrisy to accept and then inform me that you will grit your teeth and *tolerate* me I'm afraid you price your attractions right out of the market place!'

'You're being totally unreasonable... How do you expect me to feel about this situation?' Molly cried, moving after him in hot pursuit.

Sholto dealt her a shimmering smile of provocation. 'Grateful...in fact, *very* grateful that I am being this tolerant—'

'Tolerant?' Molly broke in helplessly. 'You're about as tolerant as Attila the Hun!'

Sholto discarded his shirt without comment. Molly blinked and experienced a sudden fluttering sensation in her loins that made her feel murderously uncomfortable. As she focused on the muscular breadth of his bronzed chest and the rough triangle of black curls that snaked down into an intriguing silky furrow over his flat stomach, her legs felt strangely hollow. Only as he unsnapped the waistband of his perfectly tailored trousers did she appreciate the fact that she was staring and she took a hasty step away, half turning a defensive back and then stilling again, struggling to behave as if his uninhibited ability to strip off in front of her didn't faze her in the slightest.

'Obviously I should have removed my clothes at the office...'

'Excuse me?' Molly mumbled, cheeks scarlet as she

dredged her attention hurriedly from a lean brown hip sheathed only in a slim band of black cotton.

'I gather you're staying,' Sholto murmured softly, disposing of that final item of clothing.

Clasping her damp hands together in front of her, Molly forced herself back round in his general direction, her heartbeat thudding madly somewhere in the region of her throat as she clashed for one charged second with smouldering golden eyes. Sheer undeniable panic gave her the strength to break that look first.

'I need...I need to freshen up,' she muttered, hurrying back into the sitting room to press anguished hands to her hot face in the vague hope of cooling her burning skin before she snatched up the bag containing the nightwear she had purchased.

When she returned to the bedroom, it was empty, but she could hear a shower running in one of the twin adjoining bathrooms. Involuntarily she pictured Sholto standing like a gleaming wet golden god under the water and her stomach clenched in truly terrifying reaction. In the other bathroom, behind a locked door, she undressed at the speed of a snail. She washed her face, cleaned her teeth, gargled for the first time in her life and then decided she needed a shower, a long shower, a *very* long shower...

How the heck could she walk out there and climb into that bed with him? Give herself freely without emotion or any hope of commitment? She flinched and paled. Surrender on such terms would reduce her to the level of a body he had bought. Sholto had quite deliberately stripped away any comforting pretence she might have tried to hide behind. In fact, he seemed to be reaping a punitive satisfaction from continuously underlining the fact that all he wanted was an exclusively sexual affair.

He would never know it but for once he was cherishing an utterly hopeless ambition, Molly reflected with painful self-knowledge. Emotion would be there whether he liked it or not. Sholto might never have loved her but she had never quite learned how to *stop* loving *him*. When the hatred and the bitterness had burnt out, the fascination and the hunger had remained, but she had called those feelings everything *but* love until she'd emerged from Freddy's feather bed, a sadder but infinitely wiser woman. She had melted into his arms that night as if she was living out a long-awaited fantasy and she still cringed from that awareness.

She crept out of the bathroom like a mouse hoping to evade a cat. She felt absolutely ridiculous in the thick white cotton nightdress which she had bought in such a temper. Long-sleeved and high-necked, it hung in shapeless folds around her, giving her the look of a ship in full sail. Downlighters illuminated the huge divan bed. The gleaming mahogany units on the wall opposite now stood wide, revealing an impressive array of entertainment equipment. Sholto was lying back against tumbled pillows, a single sheet drifting dangerously low on one long, powerful thigh as he caught up with the business news on television.

'Stop hovering,' he said without turning his dark head, proving that his hearing was of the most acute kind.

Molly brushed perspiring palms down over her thighs. 'What would you like me to do instead?' she enquired with rather ragged sarcasm.

Sholto's sculpted profile turned. He studied her. Incredulous dark eyes flamed gold. 'Were you planning to float around the ceiling and out the window like Mary Poppins?' he asked very drily. 'Or is there something sinuously sexy waiting to be revealed beneath all those buttons?'

'I'm afraid not.'

'Then take it off right now,' Sholto murmured with succinct bite. 'The joke's on you.'

Her breath caught in her throat, shaken green eyes colliding with unashamedly expectant gold.

'He who pays the piper calls the tune,' Sholto extended silkily. 'One of life's more basic lessons, *piccola mia*.'

'You swine,' Molly framed unsteadily, and as she spun away, excess fabric whirling round her, she caught her toes in the frilled hem of the nightdress. Stumbling, she would have lost her balance had not a powerful arm suddenly come out of nowhere to snake round her midriff in the nick of time and support her.

Above her head, Sholto expelled his breath in an audibly shaken hiss and folded her back into the hard heat of his tall, powerful body. 'You're right...but I was trying *not* to think about our wedding night...you inside that bloody bathroom refusing to come out,' he gritted. 'And then tonight you emerge after an hour and a half wearing the visual equivalent of a shroud!'

Molly's eyes had filled up with tears. She got his point even though she didn't want to. And it shook her that he recalled that ghastly night with an embittered reluctance that sounded almost equal to her own for at Freddy's house his single reference to that same occasion had been coolly derisive in content. For a split second, she let herself remain in contact with the all-male heat and strength of his muscular frame and then she forced herself to pull away.

'This isn't going to work,' she said thickly.

In answer, Sholto bent and swept her up into his arms before she could even register his intention. He settled her down on the bed, tugging the nightdress down circumspectly over her tensely extended toes. Angling a reflective look over her, his dark golden eyes suddenly

glowed with amusement and he tucked the folds round
her ankles as carefully as if he were arranging her for a
photographic session. 'Now you look like an effigy on
a medieval tomb. Beautiful and impregnable.'

'Didn't you hear what I said?' Utterly disconcerted by
his volatile change of mood, Molly lifted herself up
again, her shining russet hair tumbling in silken swathes
round her shoulders.

Sholto flipped the sheet over her as if he were putting
a small child to bed. 'First-night nerves, that's all you're
suffering from.'

'But I just can't go through with this!' Molly gasped,
desperate to make him understand that. 'It's all wrong!'

Sholto skimmed a hand up to flick a switch above the
bed and the lights dimmed to a soft, intimate level.

Molly shook her head in urgent stress of her last sen-
tence, reluctant to focus on him because she knew that
she should never have let things go so far. 'It was crazy
of me to think that I could…but then I didn't really think
about it…it was Nigel and Lena and the kids I was
thinking about…and in the heat of the moment it felt
like I had no choice…and I can't blame *you* because
you reminded me that I *did* have a choice and—'

Lean fingers slid slowly into her hair to ease her down
to him while his other hand splayed round the taut curve
of her hip to edge her closer. 'We'll talk about it in the
morning,' Sholto promised soothingly.

'But I won't be here in the morning…I need to talk
about it *now*!' Molly asserted feverishly.

'I'm listening,' Sholto pointed out, his deep dark voice
thickening and then muffling as he lifted his dark head
and pressed his mouth hotly to the tiny pulse-point flick-
ering like crazy in the hollow of her collarbone.

Molly jerked in shock from both the surprise assault
and the sensation, shivering as her spine arched and her

breasts swelled against the abrasive cotton, making her agonisingly aware of the excruciating sensitivity of her nipples. 'Don't...can't think when you do that,' she muttered disjointedly. 'And I'm trying to explain that—'

Warm hands cupped her cheekbones, long fingers brushing her hair back gently from her temples. 'We'll take it one day at a time.'

Breathlessly, Molly gazed down into fathomless pools of lambent gold, her mind suddenly dismayingly blank, a faint bemused frown pleating her brows as she struggled to recall what she had been trying to explain.

'I want you very, very much, *cara*,' Sholto murmured intently, drawing her softly down to him, running the tip of his tongue so sweetly along the compressed line of her lips that she shuddered and instinctively opened them. 'And I need you to want me the same way.'

His tongue delved into the tender interior she no longer guarded and another shiver racked her as he held her above him to play erotic games with her mouth. Her heart hammered madly, her hands dropping down to fasten to his shoulders, liquid heat rising between her quivering thighs. Then it was as if a river burst its banks inside her. Her own aching hunger washed her away. Abruptly she came down on top of him, fervently sealing her lips to his, exchanging kiss for kiss in driving, eager welcome.

Truly...madly...deeply, for ever and ever, was the last rational thought she had. He flipped her over and pinned her beneath him, a hair-roughened thigh settling between hers, and her whole body responded to the raw sensual force of that contact because all of a sudden she couldn't get close enough to him. He slid onto his side, fingers flying to the buttons on her nightdress, hands unusually clumsy, frustration currenting through him as he dragged his mouth suddenly from hers and vented a ragged expletive in Italian.

Breathing so fast her lungs felt as if they were burning, she watched him overcome the barrier, noticed his lean hands were shaking and experienced an electrifying new sense of feminine power. But then her wondering eyes were intercepted by incandescent gold and the force of her own craving made her tremble too. With an unashamed groan of need, Sholto curved his hands over the pouting white breasts he had exposed, thumbs glancing over the taut pink buds straining for his attention.

She cried out loud. He came down to her again, employed his mouth tenderly on the intolerably sensitive peaks until she writhed and clutched wildly at him, driven by a sensation far stronger than she was but still desperately wanting more. A burning, frantic ache was starting to flame low in her stomach. Her fingers clenched into his hair and then he pulled free to rise over her and crush her mouth with wild passion under his again.

And all the time his incredibly skilled hands were caressing her, smoothing possessively over her straining, acutely sensitised breasts, toying with the tormentingly tender tips and skimming down to splay over the quivering, contracting muscles of her stomach. Heart thundering insanely fast, she moaned under his wickedly expert mouth, giant waves of excitement breaking over her. Feeling the bold jut of his aroused manhood pressing against her thigh, her hips rose in wanton supplication, her knees sliding apart.

Sholto tore his lips from hers, a long shudder racking his big, powerful body as he rolled back from her, snatching in an audibly fractured breath. He groaned something in Italian and as she uttered a startled whimper of abandonment he brought her back to him, taking the invitation she offered, finally touching her where she ached to be touched and so gently and knowingly that her teeth clenched and she clung pleadingly to him in a throbbing agony of need.

'Molly...' Coiling one hand into the wild tangle of her hair, he demanded her attention when attention was the very last thing she wanted to summon.

So all-consuming was that explosive hunger for satisfaction, she did not respond. With a driven groan, Sholto withdrew his skilful fingers from the pulsing, damp centre of desire that controlled her. Bereft of sensation, her eyes opened.

'*Dio*...if you want me to stop, tell me now,' he spelt out with ragged bite. 'I won't take anything you don't want to give!'

She looked up at him, on a high of such incredible craving, it was the most extraordinary effort to try to reason. He gazed down at her on a similar high of visible frustration, a dark flush on his spectacular cheekbones, scorching golden eyes pinned to her as if she were the Holy Grail about to be snatched out of reach. Wonderment filled her as she read those unusually eloquent eyes and then a flood of fiercely possessive tenderness squeezed her heart like a gigantic hand.

She hauled him down to her again with forceful hands, raw physical hunger meshing with a new sense of freedom.

'Is that a yes...?' Sholto gritted hoarsely.

'Yes...yes...yes,' Molly mumbled, covering that beautifully tempting mouth of his worshippingly with her own.

He jerked back as if he had been prodded with a hot poker. 'Protection,' he muttered with jagged delivery.

She blinked, simply one huge, aching, mindless pool of lust, and then he returned to her, settling himself powerfully between her thighs, and she felt his smooth, hard shaft probing for entrance and simply melted. The feeling was so exquisitely pleasurable, she moaned with shock and delight. And then he was moving with hungry, driving vigour, setting up a passionate primal rhythm which sent her crazy with excitement. Their hearts thumping, pulses racing, he took her on a wild roller-coaster ride of incredible pleasure and when the sunburst explosion of release gripped her at the highest peak it was so intense, so terrifyingly strong, she wasn't capable of anything for long, endless minutes afterwards.

But she was still conscious, still capable of tensing in surprise as Sholto pressed his mouth breathlessly to hers in a fleeting, tender caress and then slid over on his side, carrying her with him. She was hot and he was even hotter but she revelled in the closeness of that embrace. And when she finally parted her lips to say his name and earned no reaction only then did she realise that Sholto had fallen asleep with a speed and lack of ceremony that reminded her disturbingly of a very young child.

Well, she had read about men doing that. He was exhausted, satiated. It was almost a relief to realise that Sholto could do something so reassuringly vulnerable and human. *Well*, she reflected again, still in a daze. He had put to flight her opposition before she'd realised what he was doing. He had advanced by subtle, nefarious means, using every trick in the book of seduction, but that meant nothing to her, not when she recalled that smouldering look of near-frantic frustration he had worn for several utterly unforgettable seconds.

Molly was still stunned by the memory of that moment. Sholto, sexually within her power, and it was a power she had not even dreamt that she possessed. So when he had said in that offhand manner at his office,

'I want you' he had really, *really* meant it but she had had to see the proof for herself to actually believe him. If anything, he had been guilty of understatement. All that sexual fire and blazing passion just for her. Finally…at last. Why he should desire her to that degree remained a mystery to Molly but evidently he hadn't been lying when he had told her that revenge had nothing to do with his demand that she live with him.

So he had ensured that she made her choice but a sense of regret remained. Nothing would ever convince her that she had made the *right* choice for herself. Hunger and love had made that decision, not intelligence. If anything she was now even more painfully aware that Sholto had the power to destroy her all over again if she wasn't careful…

Molly gave a cranky groan of complaint as she was pulled gently up against supporting pillows. Her eyes opened in amazement as a garment was dropped over her head, briefly blocking out her vision. *'What on earth…?'*

She focused wide-eyed on Sholto as he sat on the edge of the bed, helpfully slotting her arms into her nightdress as if she were a boneless rag doll. And in actual fact at that instant, as she absorbed the spectacular sizzling effect of Sholto that close, she had far more in common with that doll than she wanted to admit. Fully dressed in a sharply tailored charcoal-grey suit and smiling, he just took her breath away.

Someone knocked on the door. He sprang upright and strode to answer it. Sheer poetry in motion. Briefly, Molly closed her eyes in despair. She saw that brilliant smile again, a smile unashamedly vibrant with satisfaction, and self-loathing blossomed as she recalled the pitifully slushy feelings which had kept her glued to Sholto throughout the night hours.

'Breakfast,' Sholto announced, settling an elaborate bed tray over her knees.

Molly's nostrils flared on the unmistakable aroma of something fried and her stomach rolled instantaneously. She frowned down at the crisp meal on the plate and the most horrible heaving sensation clutched at her belly. 'Take it away!' she gulped, snaking her knees up in an awkward shimmy in an effort not to send the tray flying and then pressing her hand to her mouth in horror.

She had one brief glimpse of Sholto surveying her in appalled fascination before he reacted with commendable speed in whipping the tray out of her path. Molly flew off the bed and raced for the bathroom. Several rather unpleasant minutes followed. She was dimly aware of Sholto's presence and she absolutely did *not* want his assistance but she just couldn't get the chance to tell him that and he took charge in that infuriatingly practical fashion of his.

The sickness receded surprisingly quickly but the experience left her feeling weak. Sholto carried her back to bed with a cold damp cloth draped over her forehead. 'I've got a bug,' she lamented. 'I *hate* feeling like this...'

'*Madre di Dio...*' Sholto muttered almost inaudibly.

Molly pushed up the cloth to look at him and frowned. He was gazing out of the window but she could see the ferociously tense set of his broad shoulders beneath the fine wool of his jacket. Even as she watched he raked a restive hand through his immaculately styled black hair in a telling but unusual gesture of raw impatience.

'I should have known there was something up yesterday. I wouldn't go all dizzy over something as minor as a missed meal. Now you'll catch it,' she sighed, and a part of her thought, Serve him right.

'I don't think so…' Sholto's rich dark drawl was now coolly constrained. 'I don't think I'll catch this particular bug…'

He strolled back to the foot of the bed, dark eyes cloaked by impenetrable lashes. 'You should stay in bed for the rest of the day.'

'I'm not doing that.' Molly sat up abruptly. 'I have things to do.'

'You're a lady of leisure now.'

'A kept woman.'

The very faintest colour scored Sholto's hard cheekbones and tawny eyes suddenly shot warning flares at her. 'We're living together. That's all. There is no need to continually resurrect how we arrived at our current status.'

Bewilderment swept through Molly. Was this the same male who had gone to such derisive lengths to stress that their arrangement was nothing more than a business deal?

'I'll call you in a couple of hours and see how you're feeling,' Sholto continued, his expressive mouth compressing. 'I'm going down to Templebrooke for the weekend. I'm holding a dinner party there this evening and if you improve I would appreciate having you with me.'

He was exasperated that she was ill and might not be able to fulfil the role he had allotted to her, she gathered painfully. That was what was wrong. That was why he had that pronounced air of constraint. Knowing that irritation was both selfish and unjustifiable, he was striving to remember his manners. Molly bent her head, a lump the size of a giant rock forming at the foot of her throat.

Patently she meant nothing to Sholto unless he was physically in bed with her, having his sexual needs sat-

isfied. And of course if she was ill she might well not
be available for that role either! So doubtless her being
off-colour struck him as an unforgivable sin, most particularly on the very morning he was driving down to
see her brother and spend an absolute fortune hauling
him out of his financial mess.

'I'm sure I'll be better in time for tonight.' Drawing
in a steadying breath, she could not prevent herself from
adding, 'Please be kind to Nigel.'

A sardonic black brow rose. 'What do you think I'm
planning to do to him?'

'He's scared of you.'

'A little healthy respect won't hurt him. If there is any
backbone in Nigel, I intend to find it,' Sholto asserted
in the apparent belief that she would find that statement
reassuring. 'I'll sort him out. Don't worry about that.'

Molly could barely repress a shiver. Two more different men would have been hard to find. At thirty-one,
Sholto was only three years older than Nigel. But Sholto
was naturally tough and self-assured while her brother's
confidence had been destroyed by the constant bullying,
criticism and contempt he had received from their stepfather while he was growing up.

Molly linked her hands together as he reached the
door. 'What are you going to tell Nigel about us?' she
asked tightly.

'That we're together again...what else?' Sholto responded with deflating speed, as if the matter were too
utterly obvious and trivial to require any further thought.

'Together again'. What a description; what a simplis-
tic male evasion of reality! As the door closed on Sholto,
Molly slid gingerly out of bed and studied herself in a
mirror. A mistress, a kept woman. It didn't matter that
she loved him, didn't make any difference that she
wanted him as much as he appeared to want her. There

was nothing equal, secure or caring about a relationship in which sex was the sole means of intimacy and money the sole reason for its existence.

Abruptly the door burst open again. Sholto paused on the threshold. 'I forgot to mention this earlier. I *like* the way you look.'

She was jolted by his sudden reappearance and her eyes were wide with confusion. 'I beg your pardon?'

Stunning dark eyes clashed warningly with hers. 'If you change the colour of your hair, have it all cut off or start starving yourself into doll-sized dresses again, I will go stark staring mad! I don't want you to change yourself...it was a total and complete turn-off the last time!'

Transfixed by that abrasive assurance, Molly whispered, 'Really?'

'I didn't say anything because I didn't want to hurt your feelings.'

It went without saying that he wasn't concerned about hurting her feelings now.

'I was halfway into the limo before it occurred to me that you might start reinventing yourself again,' Sholto imparted with a barely concealed recoil at the prospect.

Long after he had gone, Molly studied the space where he had been. 'A total and complete turn-off'. It was so deeply ironic when she recalled how frantically hard she had struggled to improve her appearance. And he had actually liked her the way she *was*? Was that possible? Long straight hair, hardly any make-up, generous breasts and hips and precious little interest in being fashionable. The knowledge that a male as supremely sophisticated as Sholto could have preferred her that way shook Molly inside out.

All the women she had met in his circle had dressed and looked like models, every inch of them artificially enhanced, every one of them thin. They had talked constantly about the latest beauty treatments, who had or had not had cosmetic surgery, the benefits of collagen for lips, liposuction for thighs. Molly had cowered like an ugly duckling in their midst, trying not to cringe every time some female pointedly told her about a good diet and exercise programme. She could even recall Pandora gently suggesting that she consider a breast-reduction operation.

Even more ironically, she now looked very much as she had looked when Sholto had first met her four and a half years ago. Slowly she shook her head. From the minute they had got engaged, she registered, she had unwittingly begun eradicating everything which had originally attracted him to her...

Templebrooke House in Surrey had been the ancestral home of the Brooke family for almost three hundred years. Sholto's mother, Olivia, had been a Brooke, the elder of two daughters, and she had inherited the magnificent eighteenth-century Palladian mansion from her father. Set in the rolling acres of a lush, tree-dotted estate, Templebrooke had survived only because Olivia had married money. Her younger sister, Meriel, had copied her example and had given birth to a baby girl when Sholto was two years old. That little girl had been Pandora.

Uneasily conscious of how late she was and of how completely she had ignored Sholto's autocratic instructions on the phone mid-morning, and resenting her own unease as much as she had resented being told what to do with her day, Molly climbed out of her little hatchback and began to extract her cases from the boot.

Ogden surged down the steps, looking most relieved to see her. 'No, madam...really, madam,' he scolded gently. 'Someone else will deal with your luggage.'

With pronounced reluctance, Molly entered the great house. Pandora's presence had ruined her only previous visit to Templebrooke. Indeed Templebrooke had long lived in her memory as the backdrop against which Pandora looked most at home, playing the role of blue-blooded society hostess with a panache that few could have equalled and certainly not a twenty-year-old typist raised in a country vicarage to bake buns and blend in with the woodwork.

Sholto was already crossing the magnificent hall to meet her, golden eyes brilliant with exasperation. 'Where have you been all day? You left the house long before Ogden did and he arrived hours ago!'

'I got on the train and went home to pack,' Molly admitted grudgingly.

'Our guests will be arriving within forty minutes.'

Our, she noted—clearly a slip of the tongue since she hadn't a clue who he was entertaining and was utterly dreading the incredulity which would be the inevitable result of her sudden reappearance in Sholto's life.

'It won't take me long to get changed...particularly when you made such a point about preferring me not to gild the lily,' Molly said thinly.

'I had a selection of clothes sent down from London for you,' Sholto informed her drily, ignoring the gibe. 'There was no need for you to go home. Ogden has already made arrangements for professional packers to clear your apartment. Everything would've been taken care of for you.'

Molly stiffened and visibly bristled. She had given her landlady a month's notice, had packed her clothes and contrived to box the remainder of her possessions. She would scarcely have believed it possible to do as much as she had managed to do within the few hours at her disposal. Doing those things for herself had given her a sense of being in control of her life again. But Sholto had just exposed that feeling for the fallacy it was. She was not in control...*he* was.

'I'm putting my whole life on hold while I'm with you. Isn't that enough? Can't I even be left to sort out the life I'm being forced to leave behind?' she demanded sharply.

Before she could sidestep him to head for the stairs, Sholto curved a lean hand round her elbow to still her again. 'How are you feeling?'

Surprised that he hadn't challenged her angry response, she compressed her lips. 'I'm feeling fine.'

'If you're feeling even slightly unwell, there is no need for you to put in an appearance tonight.'

'I'm perfectly all right.'

His beautiful mouth tightened, dark eyes narrowing. '*Dio*...I didn't know where you were... I was worried about you!'

Had he been worried that she had gone for good? Reneged on their *business* deal? Short-changed him with one brief night? As far as Molly was concerned, he had no rights outside his own bedroom door. He had made the rules and he hadn't mentioned anything about policing her every movement.

'And you shouldn't be raving about the countryside tiring yourself out,' Sholto continued grimly. 'You look exhausted.'

'This is about control, isn't it?' Molly accused. 'I walked out of the town house without saying where I was going. I got on a train instead of getting into one of your cars—'

'No, this isn't about control, Molly,' Sholto drawled softly. 'It relates to good manners and consideration for others and you behaving like a very stubborn child.'

Mortified by the retaliation, Molly gave him a furious

look and whirled away to start up the stairs. But as she climbed her steps grew gradually slower and slower...

All the way up that sweeping staircase, Molly found herself staring at the huge portrait on the landing. It depicted Olivia and her sister, Meriel, as debutantes. Both tall, blonde and classically beautiful. One had to look beyond Sholto's dramatically dark colouring to see the resemblance but his aristocratic nose, finely modelled mouth and high cheekbones were all undeniably attributes from his mother's side of the family.

On the other side of the landing hung an equally large and dominating portrait of Sholto's father, Riccardo Cristaldi. Dark and dynamically attractive, he had been a notoriously unfaithful husband. The artist had captured the element of raw, earthy sexuality which had stamped those hard features. Molly had spent years striving pointlessly to recall those three faces, setting them next to an image of Pandora and Sholto in her mind's eye...and constantly replaying seemingly quite innocent comments and pieces of information she had picked up during their engagement:

'They're touchingly close for cousins, don't you think?'

'Pandora might as well be joined to Sholto at the hip...but he doesn't seem to object.'

'I always believed they would marry—'

'Never—they behave more like brother and sister.'

'One wonders, doesn't one?' A silence and a long look of shared and malicious amusement.

'Meriel *did* make a dead set at Riccardo when they first met...but there was never any doubt about which sister he would marry when Olivia was to inherit Templebrooke.'

'Riccardo had tremendous charm.'

'Meriel married that boring little banker, Parker

Stevenson, on the rebound…and surely you remember how that business ended? Several years after she died, Parker shot himself and nobody could ever work out *why*. He was the most devoted father and Pandora was only sixteen. She was completely distraught. She was in Italy with Sholto for months afterwards.'

'Perhaps Parker found out something that made life seem no longer worth living…'

Those snatches of conversation had haunted Molly ever since she'd made that first appalling leap in comprehension, seeing a connection, initially drawing back from it in stricken disbelief. But the more she had matched that suspicion to the facts, the more neatly they had seemed to dovetail. And things that hadn't really made sense before had suddenly come together with chilling, striking clarity…

CHAPTER SEVEN

MOLLY wriggled and twisted awkwardly in front of the elegant cheval-glass. She heard the door opening at the far end of the superbly furnished bedroom and didn't bother to turn her head. Sholto appeared in her reflection and cool, sure hands detached hers from the recalcitrant zip.

'You look fabulous.' As he dealt with the zip, he pressed his lips caressingly to the soft skin of one pale shoulder.

Molly wasn't quick enough to suppress the responsive shiver that racked her but she wasn't in any mood to be reminded of their intimacy. Everywhere she looked and everything she touched drove that point home hard. Within twenty-four hours, Sholto had blown life as she knew it apart. She was unemployed. She had become a bird of passage without roots. And all for what? The lustful whim of a rogue male accustomed to satisfying his every whim. And he would dispense with her services the minute he got bored with her in bed.

But here she was for the moment, sheathed in a short sleek designer dress the exact shade of burnished copper. In a million years, she could never have afforded to buy such a dress for herself. It annoyed her even more that the style and the colour were tremendously flattering and that it fitted like a glove. Tonight she would be paraded like a glossy possession for people to stare at and all the women would take one look and know that *he* had paid for the dress!

She stuffed her feet into the toning court shoes and

ran a brisk brush through the shining fall of her hair, murderously conscious of Sholto's contemplative scrutiny.

'You were still sleeping in my arms when I woke up this morning. What has changed since then?' he enquired levelly.

Irrational rage that he had woken up first and surprised her in that position assailed Molly. It was all right to be a little weak when he wasn't aware of it, utter stupidity to let him see that weakness. He was no fool. If she was even slightly clingy, he would soon suspect that she was an even bigger idiot than she herself thought she was. How could she possibly love a man who was reducing her to this level?

'Molly…' Sholto prompted. 'I would appreciate an answer.'

She whirled round, green eyes on fire with angry defensiveness. 'An explanation would be pointless. I doubt that you give a damn what people think!'

He frowned. 'What are you talking about?'

'All of a sudden I come out of nowhere again and here I am *living* with you!'

She whirled away again, annoyed that she had exposed her embarrassment to that extent. Straight back in the door and straight into bed with him. That was what people were going to think. And she wasn't looking forward to meeting the amused and speculative eyes of those who would find their renewed togetherness as highly entertaining as it was strange.

'So you still make a great white god of appearances,' Sholto derided. 'I have no time for that, particularly when I'm aware that if it hadn't been for the misleading appearance of events four years ago our marriage might still be intact.'

Her breath caught in her throat at the charge. 'There was nothing misleading about those events...'

'You condemned me on the strength of a picture in a newspaper. Why? Because it made you look foolish, because you were obsessively jealous of Pandora and your narrow little mind could not comprehend that sex is not the dominating factor of *every* relationship between a man and a woman.' His lean, strong face was set in lines of unconcealed contempt.

The silence pounded. Molly had flushed with incredulous outrage and pain that he should even have dared to mention *that* name again. It was like a red rag to a bull and just about everything he'd said beyond that name escaped her.

'I was not obsessively jealous of that bitch!' she blazed, with a sudden shudder of utterly uncontrollable fury. 'I put up with her for months without a murmur of complaint. I was a complete wimp. I put up with being shoved into a back seat for the whole of our engagement and upstaged at every turn. For *your* sake, I put up with all her sweet little barbs about how overweight I was, how badly dressed, how totally unsuitable I was to be your wife! Yes, I may have started out feeling jealous but, believe me, at the end of the day I just plain hated her guts!'

Sholto had turned pale beneath his sun-bronzed skin. Shock that she should have dared to attack so openly, she surmised, and bitter anger on his precious Pandora's behalf. She was trembling, shattered by her own outburst but in retrospect not prepared to retract a word. Perhaps it was time Sholto was made to realise that she was not the naive and blind little fool she had once been.

His brilliant dark eyes were as hard as diamonds. 'Pandora was—'

Molly spread her hands in a staying gesture of very

real warning. 'Just you say her name one more time to me and I walk out of here. And don't throw Nigel at me because I won't listen, I won't hear, I'll be *gone*!' she asserted with fierce conviction. 'I will not tolerate that woman anywhere near me, so you had better keep her well out of my way!'

'That shouldn't be too difficult,' Sholto retorted with icy, deflating cool. 'She lives in New York now.'

Molly spun away from him, her stomach twisting. He probably flew to New York at least once a month. But then they would *have* to be more discreet now. That story her friend, Jenna, had given to the Press had ripped the lid off any pretence that Sholto and Pandora were only platonic friends. But the pair of them had got off lightly, she reflected painfully. They had only stood accused of having an affair behind Molly's back. And that had shocked those who knew them but it hadn't shocked them half as much as the *whole* truth would have done. And even now she was grateful that that truth had not been revealed. She had never been able to feel compassion for Pandora. That would have been asking too much. But she cared enough about Sholto to want to protect him from the kind of sordid scandal that would follow him the rest of his days.

'I am very angry with you,' Sholto delivered with murderous quietness into the thundering, dragging silence, golden eyes ice-cold. 'In fact, I am so angry I could quite happily throw you out of this house.'

Tears scorched Molly's eyes. Her mouth wobbled and then tightened again as she fought to stem all the wild emotions still clamouring for exit inside her. Anger, resentment, frustration and fierce, bitter pain. 'Just say the word and I'm out of here!'

She waited, desperately wanting him to say that word

and forcibly free her from her own emotional enslavement.

An ebony brow rose. 'You can't manipulate me like that.'

She bent her head at the warning, biting down hard on the soft underside of her lip. Sometimes he read her mind so easily, it scared her to think what else he might know.

'And before we close the subject of the shortest marriage on public record permit me to say this one thing.'

Molly's chin came up. 'Say what you like.'

Sholto gazed back at her from the door. 'When I would have defended myself, you wouldn't give me the opportunity and I think that the last thing you deserve right now is an explanation.'

Particularly when the challenge of coming up with any remotely viable explanation would have taxed Machiavelli, she completed for herself. The door closed. No way would he ever tell her the truth. He would lie. He would *have* to lie. He would have no choice. Some things weren't acceptable even in this day and age. And she knew him well enough to understand exactly how it had happened and exactly why it had happened.

Pandora was the one woman Sholto couldn't have. And yet in every way she was his perfect match. They had spent little time in each other's company while they were children. Pandora had been brought up in England, Sholto in Italy. They had been teenagers before they'd become close. Had the attraction been instantaneous or something that crept up on them both without warning? Had they known even then that it could never be? Was that why they had been so scrupulously careful not to let others suspect? Was that why both of them had always had other relationships?

She knew she was torturing herself and she snatched

in a slow, deep breath, deliberately blanking out her mind and calming herself down. Then she walked forward to the mirror. As she smoothed a slight crease out of the bodice on her dress, she grimaced at the tenderness of her breasts. Of course it was about that time of the month, wasn't it? She frowned and thirty seconds later she was checking her diary.

So her period was late. That was unusual, *very* unusual, but then the last weeks had been pretty stressful. A slight chill quivered down her spine, inner anxiety ready to explode. That tummy upset had been a coincidence, that was all. Sholto would *never* have taken a risk like that. A male as essentially cool, controlled and logical as he was would not engage in unprotected sex.

Comforted by that staunch conviction, she opened the door and then it occurred to her that no method of contraception was foolproof and that accidents did happen. Please, not *me*, she thought fearfully, her blood running cold again with panic.

All the way down the stairs Molly attempted to rehearse a casual, artless question which she could hopefully throw in his general direction without sounding either foolish or paranoid.

'You wouldn't have been stupid enough to—?' No, that wouldn't do.

'By the way, is there a possibility—?' No, that gave away too much, underlined the mortifying fact that she had been totally detached from intelligence herself that night.

Sholto was in the vast drawing room chatting to a man and a woman. Molly hovered just inside the door. Sholto crossed the great sea of Aubusson carpet, a social smile skimming his mouth, his compelling dark eyes wintercool. Molly decided without much difficulty to put off the awkward question indefinitely and looked away, simultaneously meeting the astonished but delighted smile of the blonde woman as she turned round. Recognising the couple, Molly moved forward to greet them with genuine pleasure. 'Natalie...Gerald, how are you?'

'Thunderstruck to find you here,' Natalie confided with frank amusement when the men had drifted away again. 'Sholto only invited us this morning. He said he had a stodgy bunch of business acquaintances dining here tonight but that he had a very special reason for asking us over. Now I feel flattered. You and I always did get on well, didn't we?'

'Believe me, I'm grateful to see a familiar face.' Molly laughed, rather struck by the idea that Sholto had invited Natalie for her benefit. She had been able to relax with the other woman from the first moment they'd met over four years ago.

'But you must be extremely happy not to see one particular face,' the blonde remarked meaningfully. 'Dare I ask if you will be attending the wedding?'

Molly's facial muscles had stiffened at that apparent allusion to Pandora but now her eyes betrayed her confusion. 'Sorry...what wedding?'

'Pandora's...didn't you know? She's getting married this summer.'

In shock, Molly turned pale as milk but she kept her slight smile in place. Natalie was very nice but she was also a notorious gossip. 'Who's the lucky man?'

'A very handsome Brazilian multimillionaire. I understand she's completely besotted with him. I do find *that* hard to imagine. It was always the other way round for her. But then we haven't seen her in years. She disappeared off the scene not very long after you did.'

With an unsteady hand, Molly reached for the drink Ogden extended to her on a silver tray. Pandora was in love and soon to be married. It sounded almost too good to be true. As quickly, Sholto's renewed interest in Molly herself made the very worst kind of demeaning sense. At her lowest ebb four years ago, she had come to the conclusion that her sole attraction in Sholto's eyes could only have been the complete impossibility of her *ever* reminding him of the woman he loved. She would never launch a thousand ships, she thought bitterly, but possibly Sholto found her very ordinariness a soothing contrast.

Sholto curved a light arm round her back and eased her forward to meet the latest arrivals. She smiled and chatted, hadn't a clue what she said. As they moved on, Sholto angled his dark head down to her. 'I hope you don't mind drinking mineral water. You looked so tired earlier, I was afraid alcohol might send you to sleep.'

Molly hadn't even noticed what she was drinking but now a flush of chagrined remembrance lit her cheeks. She would never, ever forget Sholto accusing her of being drunk on their wedding night. 'Or maybe you were afraid I would fall into the soup and embarrass you!'

'Nothing embarrasses me, but since you do not rejoice in that same indifference I suggest that you take a deep breath and control that temper. To be frank, my patience is wearing thin, *cara*.'

Once, when Sholto had turned to ice it had made her feel crushed and despised. But she was four years older now and tonight she was a stormy sea of violently conflicting emotions. She pictured him earlier, coldly outraged by her abuse of Pandora. She recalled their wedding night, the desperate courage it had taken to try and confront him. But in the end it had been sheer black comedy, she conceded wretchedly. She had been in such a state by the time she finally let him into that bedroom, she had been virtually incoherent with the extremity of her distress. And then the phone had rung. Within thirty seconds he had been striding towards the door.

'I'm afraid I have to go out,' Sholto had announced, shooting her a grim backward glance. 'But then it wouldn't be much of a party staying home with a hysterical, raving, drunken bride. I'll tell Ogden to send up some coffee.'

And she had sobbed, screamed, shouted, screeched all the way down to the ground floor in his wake but nothing she had done or said had made the slightest impression on his determination to depart and to do so at all possible speed. With the hindsight of greater maturity, Molly appreciated for the first time that she had really done everything possible to drive him out of that door.

Now, in the magnificent dining room, she found herself seated at the very foot of the table with Sholto sixteen place settings away at the head. It was like being exiled, punished by deprivation. But, secure in the knowledge that they were in the midst of a running battle because she was not doing what he expected and backing down, Molly was determined not to betray her vulnerability.

'I take it that you're the mistress of the house,' the suave young banker seated beside her drawled with a loud chuckle at his own unamusing wit.

'Gosh, that's funny!' Molly giggled like a choking drain, colour staining her cheeks. 'I haven't heard anything that funny in ages!'

Her companion did not realise that she was joking. He shifted closer and for the remainder of that interminable meal bored her to death with stories of his greatest moments hunting, shooting and fishing. She hung on his every word because Sholto was watching her. Something Donald had once said to her sprang to mind. 'He winds you up like a battery toy and then he leaves you flailing...' With a repressed shiver, she finally fell silent over the coffee-cups, acknowledging that she had been guilty of pathetically childish, attention-seeking behaviour. She all but shrank when the banker pressed his business card into her hand and urged her to contact him when she was 'free'.

'Sholto's in a very strange mood this evening,' Natalie whispered well over an hour after Molly had stopped even looking in that direction. 'And I would have to say that, although I have never seen him lose his temper, tonight may well be the night, Molly.'

Molly screened a yawn. She was exhausted. Even as Ogden closed the door on the last guest, she was proceeding like a sleepwalker towards the stairs. Sholto caught her back, slid one powerful arm behind her knees and the other round her back and swept her smoothly up into his arms.

'Were you feeling neglected over dinner?'

Molly toyed with the idea of objecting to being carried and then measured the incredible length of the staircase and subsided. 'Excuse me?'

'All that frantic schoolgirlish giggling and batting of your eyelashes. It wasn't exactly subtle.'

'Subtle would've been wasted on him. And he was very taken with me,' Molly mumbled round another huge yawn. 'Obviously he likes frantically giggly tarts.'

'Sharing my bed does not make you a tart!' Sholto bit down at her, his arms tightening round her.

'What do you call a woman who sleeps with a man for money?'

'What the hell's got into you?' Sholto launched down at her rawly.

Molly gazed up at him drowsily. Dear heaven, even

on the brink of a rage he looked so good he churned her up inside.

'*Dio*...you've been behaving like a maniac ever since I left you this morning!'

'It's called doing my own thing. You do it all the time. But you can't stand it when anybody else does it.'

'I didn't bring you back into my life to do your own thing,' Sholto gritted with unapologetic candour.

'Of course not.' Molly let her limbs sink into the wonderfully comfortable mattress he had laid her down on. 'But you misjudged your victim.'

'Meaning?'

'I'm as stubborn as you are...I always was.'

He flipped her over with surprising gentleness and pulled down the zip on her dress. 'It's as if half of you wants to be here and the other half doesn't.'

Molly froze, her drowsiness driven back by the disturbing depth of his perception.

'It's as if you will do and say anything to keep me at a distance. And tonight it worked,' Sholto imparted drily. '*Buonanotte, cara.*'

Molly rolled over in astonishment and watched him stride fluidly out of the room. His ability to sidestep conflict and take her by surprise shook her. But then that aspect of Sholto had always intimidated her. The unexpected was the norm for him. And instead of feeling relieved that he was leaving her alone to sleep elsewhere Molly felt rejected and was furious with herself when she ended up tossing and turning in the giant canopied bed, unable to find the sleep that she knew she needed.

She hadn't even asked him about Nigel. But then she knew she didn't need to. Sholto would keep the promises he had made. She had absolutely no doubt about that. Sholto was famous for straight dealing in the business world. Nigel and Lena and the children would be secure but they were no longer the driving force behind her turmoil. Molly was infinitely more worried about herself. And what if by some ghastly trick of fate she *was* pregnant?

At eight the following morning she got out of bed. She felt nauseous again but at least she wasn't sick. Her cases had been unpacked the night before and her clothes now hung in the spacious dressing-room units but there was no male apparel beside them. This was not, as she had assumed, Sholto's bedroom. Pulling on jeans and a shirt, she looked at herself in the bathroom mirror.

Shadowed eyes, pallid cheeks. She looked awful but she would feel infinitely better after she had purchased one of those home-testing pregnancy kits. Because it was almost certain she was worrying over nothing. In fact she was probably a classic case of a woman who had been reckless convinced that retribution in the way of an unplanned baby was coming her way. Gosh, she couldn't even *imagine* being pregnant!

An hour and a half later Molly sat staring at the test kit she had rushed out to buy as if concentrated mental imaging might miraculously change the result. She pushed a shaking hand through her hair and jerkily released her breath.

Ogden knocked on the bedroom door to inform her that Sholto was waiting for her to come downstairs and have breakfast with him. Molly took fifteen minutes to gather up the strength.

Sholto was in the morning room—an only slightly cosier version of the grand dining room. As she entered he stood up and she wondered starkly if those superb manners would carry him smoothly through what she had to tell him. He was wearing close-fitting cream jodhpurs and a black sweater. Her heart banged feverishly fast behind her breastbone. Even in the grip of sick, high-wire tension, just looking at Sholto turned her bones to water. Her wavering lower limbs forced her somewhat clumsily down into a chair.

'I was in the stable yard when you drove off before nine. I was surprised to see you up that early,' Sholto commented as Ogden served them both from the magnificent Georgian sideboard which bore a selection of breakfast dishes.

'I had an errand to do,' Molly muttered tautly.

To satisfy Ogden, she accepted a cup of coffee and some toast while Sholto was served with a cooked breakfast that would have killed a less healthy male specimen. Ogden departed at a stately pace and the door closed.

She sugared her coffee and kept on stirring. The prospect of telling Sholto loomed like a hangman's noose before her. It would be horribly humiliating. Sholto was not easily shocked but *this* was something else again. He would be shattered and how could she blame him? One time, just one time, and for her the very first time...

'Are you thinking of emptying the entire sugar bowl into that cup?' Sholto enquired lazily, almost gently.

Molly dropped the teaspoon with a clatter back on the saucer and lifted her head. 'I'm pregnant...' she framed tightly.

Brilliant dark eyes rested on her strained face and unwittingly frightened eyes. It was a slow, steady appraisal. He didn't blink, nor did his expression alter even by a degree.

Molly breathed shakily, 'Sholto...did you hear what I said?'

'I was waiting to see if you were planning to add anything else,' Sholto confessed, and he started pouring himself a cup of coffee with a hand as steady as a rock. 'But I should have known better. You had to sit there looking at me as if you expected me to lunge across the table at you and say that if you were pregnant it was nothing to do with me!'

Completely disconcerted by the direction the dialogue was taking, Molly gaped at him in bewilderment.

Sholto coiled back fluidly into his chair, dark, dark eyes semi-screened by his lush lashes. 'There's no need for melodrama, Molly. And I can't fake shock when I already suspected that you might be pregnant.'

Molly frowned. 'But how *could* you have suspected? I only started worrying last night.'

'I took a calculated risk that night at Freddy's,' Sholto admitted very quietly, watching her eyes widen in shock. 'So you *didn't* register that fact. I did wonder and I did intend to mention it the next morning, but some-how...that didn't quite pan out, any more than my call at your office did.'

Colour had surged into Molly's cheeks again and incredulity fired her gaze as she stared back at him. 'Are you saying that you didn't take any precautions?' she prompted, dry-mouthed with disbelief.

'You were there, Molly,' Sholto countered.

'I wasn't sure, I just assumed...I just blasted well didn't notice!' Molly vented in a sudden shrill burst as she planted her hands on the table-edge and leapt furiously upright. The light-headed sensation which afflicted her only made her angrier. 'I can't believe that you could be that irresponsible...that selfish...that *inexcusably* careless—'

'Sit down and eat your toast,' Sholto advised flatly.

She sat down again only because she was dizzy. Every trace of her earlier anxiety and embarrassment had been banished by his confession but she was in the grip of the most devastating sense of shock.

'*Dio*...I don't have one-night stands and I had nothing

with me. It was that simple. I took the risk but you took it with me—'

'You utter toad!' Molly condemned, infuriated by his attitude. 'You knew perfectly well that I didn't know what I was doing!'

'*Santo cielo!*' His lean, strong face revealing his exasperation, Sholto threw his hands in the air in a gesture of stark frustration. 'What does it matter *how* it happened? You're expecting my child now. Let us deal with that. It is a waste of time to wrangle about anything else!'

'And you kept quiet too…' Molly thought back to the previous day, his constraint, his assertion that he would not catch that particular bug, and her stomach twisted. She had watched him go pale in his office when she'd felt faint, recognised his grim tension when she was ill. She hadn't known it but she had been receiving his true reaction then. And it had not been today's cool, collected calm.

'I saw no reason to worry you unnecessarily—'

'*Unnecessarily?*' she queried chokily.

'We were both going to know soon enough. Talking about it wasn't going to take the possibility away. Apportioning blame is equally pointless. This is a time to be constructive, rather than *de*structive.'

But Molly was too upset for that. Right from the start Sholto had known that he might make her pregnant. His damnable arrogance! He had computed the risk, taken the chance, had undoubtedly expected his legendary good luck to hold. But it *hadn't*. A shock of no mean proportions to a male like Sholto Cristaldi. Recalling his conspicuous lack of nonchalance the day before, Molly could not be fooled by his present calm response.

'You want me to be constructive?' Her voice shook at the suggestion.

'This *is* a mutual responsibility.'

But it was her body, her life, her future which had been irrevocably changed, not his. That there could actually be a baby growing inside her still felt unreal. In the simmering silence, Sholto rang for Ogden and ordered a fresh pot of coffee.

'Obviously we have a lot to discuss,' he drawled with that same maddening cool.

Her hands tightly linked on her lap below the level of the table, Molly looked up, her heart-shaped face tense and drawn. 'I'm not having a termination. I'm sorry but that isn't open for discussion.'

His stunning dark eyes narrowed. 'Did I suggest that it might be?'

'You couldn't help but see that as the most convenient solution,' Molly muttered, running an unsteady hand through her mane of russet hair. 'After all, this baby wasn't conceived in a relationship. It's the accidental consequence of a one-night stand.'

'I would not have suggested an abortion,' Sholto countered with cold clarity. 'Nor would I refer to that distinctly cathartic encounter at Freddy's as a one-night stand.'

Recalling that same encounter, Molly refused to look at him. Tears were stinging the back of her eyes, her throat thickening. 'Frankly,' she enunciated with difficulty, 'I don't want to even think about that night, never mind talk about it.'

A dark flush scored the slashing lines of his cheekbones. 'Molly—'

'*Please,*' she cut in jaggedly.

Without warning, he thrust back his chair and sprang upright. Out of the corner of her eye, she watched him pace over to the tall windows, his seething tension palpable now. 'You know that I have always wanted children...'

'Yes.' He would have had to strain his ears to catch that concession. Molly didn't require the reminder that once he had been prepared to marry her to gain those children while conserving his heart, his thoughts and his emotions for another woman. And even more clearly did she recall that before that wedding he had been careful to suggest that they didn't wait too long to start a family.

'Naturally, I want *this* child,' Sholto completed almost aggressively.

Molly curved her arms around herself as if she was cold. All of a sudden she *knew* what was coming next, marvelled that she had not foreseen it from the outset. She stared at the table until it blurred. 'I know what you're going to say...please don't say it.'

'Since when did you read my mind?' But he was off balance. She could hear it. His accent growled along every syllable, so sinfully sexy it made her stupid heart pound.

She forced her head up, her gaze angrily accusing, revealing nothing of the bitter pain of rejection she was experiencing. 'You're about to ask me to marry you because you want the baby. And my answer to that is...no!'

Ebony lashes dropped low on his spectacular dark eyes, his vibrant features freezing. *'No?'*

CHAPTER EIGHT

A HYSTERICAL laugh lurked like a dangerous tripwire low in Molly's dry throat. Sholto was striving so hard to contain his disbelief. And she really couldn't blame him, could she? The last time he had asked her to marry him she had been ecstatic and would never have countenanced a less conventional arrangement. And now she was living under his roof, sharing his bed and pregnant and he just could not comprehend her negative response.

'You've been acting really strangely since yesterday. I'm not being sexist here but I suspect it's something to do with your hormones,' Sholto drawled with deflating superiority.

The laugh escaped against Molly's volition and she crammed a hand against her tremulous mouth, terrified that a sob would follow.

'If you can find something amusing in all this, share it with me!' Sholto invited with raw bite.

Molly shook her head urgently, not trusting herself to speak.

Why had she been afraid that an abortion would be his first request? How utterly blind she had been! He had been looking after his baby with tender loving care from the instant he'd suspected its existence! Telling her to stay in bed, not to tire herself out, steering her clear of alcohol. Sholto had come to terms with the situation by focusing on the one positive aspect he saw...he had *always* wanted a child.

And now, seen in that light, with the promise of a profitable gain in the offing, an inconvenient pregnancy suddenly became acceptable! After all, what did he have to lose? The woman he loved was far away and would soon be another man's wife. But Molly was bitterly aware that if she married Sholto she would not only be second best to Pandora, she would also end up being second best to her own child in his eyes. No, she thought fiercely, she had no plans to submit herself for use as a brood mare! It would be the ultimate humiliation to live with the knowledge that that was the only reason he had married her.

'You are the last woman in the world I can imagine looking forward to life as an unmarried mother,' Sholto spelt out grimly.

She wasn't looking forward to it at all, but a shotgun marriage on his cold-blooded terms appealed even less. 'You can't buy my baby with a wedding ring,' Molly told him, experiencing a surge of bitter satisfaction at that awareness.

'You are not behaving like a rational woman.'

'You've got no right to complain about that. A rational woman would never have ended up in bed with you in the first place!' Molly retorted with fierce self-loathing.

The silence with which he greeted that assurance seemed to last for ever.

'So...' Sholto finally breathed. 'What *are* your plans?'

Molly stilled, shaken by that simple question. As yet she had not thought beyond the immediate present. 'I haven't really had time to make any...but obviously I'll move out as soon as possible—'

'*Madre di Dio*...you are not leaving with my baby inside you!' Sholto grated in a savage undertone.

Shaken by that aggressiveness, Molly flinched. 'You don't own me.'

'But I do virtually own your brother,' Sholto reminded her with chilling clarity.

'Don't you think you've done enough damage?' Molly condemned raggedly as she stood up. 'Isn't it enough that you've wrecked my life?'

A tiny muscle pulled tight at the corner of his compressed lips, accentuating the pallor below his sunbronzed skin. 'We have an agreement *and* a relationship and you are not walking out of either, Molly.'

Just one word, just one look and she wouldn't even have thought about leaving but Sholto had made not one single emotional reference. He had centred his entire focus on the baby, not on *her*. Throat working like mad to hold back a sob, Molly headed for the door.

'Where are you going?'

'To visit my family.'

'I'll take you,' Sholto asserted smoothly.

'No, thanks,' she said chokily.

'Then you go in the limo.'

Since she was on the very brink of bursting into tears, she didn't argue, just walked on out into the hall.

'You have to leave right now?' Expelling his breath in an exasperated hiss, Sholto told Ogden to have the limousine brought round and then he swung back to her. 'If you're not home by ten this evening, I'll come and fetch you.'

'Why?' Molly asked thickly but with considerable venom. 'Do you think the baby needs an early night?'

Sholto ground out an Italian expletive and without the smallest advance warning of his intention hauled her rigid, resisting body to him with two fiercely determined hands. His fingers came up to push up her chin so that he could see her face and she tried to fight that too, a tidal wave of emotions threatening her as she jerked her head mutinously away.

But a controlling hand meshed into her hair and his hot, hungry mouth found hers. That thunderous collision sent a shock wave sizzling right down to Molly's toes. She swayed and he caught her up against him, prising her lips apart with raw, demanding force. It was like being hit by a lightning bolt. She clutched at his shoulders, swept away by that wildly passionate kiss. And a split second later she was free, blinking bemusedly, aching all over with the intensity of her arousal.

'I think that *you* are more in need of the early night,' Sholto delivered drily.

Burning with chagrined colour and completely unable to meet the derision in those shrewd golden eyes, Molly pelted out to the limousine as if she were being pursued by a hungry tiger.

The first thing she noticed when she entered her brother's house was the gleaming tidiness of the kitchen. Normality had been restored. Turning from the sink, Lena looked delighted to see her and instantly called out, 'Nigel? Molly's here!'

Then she closed her arms round Molly in a fierce hug that said it all.

'Nigel's going to get some training in one of Sholto's companies,' Lena explained then. 'So for the next nine months at least he'll be commuting…'

Nigel appeared in the doorway. 'Sholto's sending me back to school,' he said with a rueful twist of his mouth. 'I didn't fancy the idea much when he first mentioned it but he's never going to agree to me managing the garden centre again if I can't prove I'm capable of doing it right.'

'You *are* capable,' Molly told him.

'We're getting a mortgage on the house.' Nigel straightened his thin shoulders. 'Lena and I insisted on that. That should take care of the other debts we have.

Sholto will be forking out enough without having to settle them as well.'

'Sholto was really nice,' Lena told her shyly. 'I never, ever would've thought he could be that nice.'

Nigel nodded. 'He was. He sort of unbent and talked to the kids and stuff because... Hell, I nearly died when I saw him at the front door!'

Lena gave Molly a coy, admiring look. 'Imagine you not letting on what a romantic time you had when you got snowed in with him.'

Involuntarily, a bitter laugh was dredged from Molly. 'I didn't get romance, I got pregnant!'

Nigel and Lena gaped at her with wide eyes and open mouths.

Molly flushed brick-red and spun away. 'I can't believe I just said that...'

Lena cleared her throat awkwardly. 'So you'll be getting married, then,' she assumed.

'Obviously she'll be getting married,' Nigel told his wife.

'Well, actually no...I won't be,' Molly said stiffly.

The silence behind her lingered a long time.

'It's hard to picture Sholto getting married because he *has* to get married,' Lena conceded heavily.

'Yeah, well...it is kind of hard,' Nigel muttered in grudging agreement. 'I mean, let's face it, there's nothing cool about a shotgun do, is there? But it doesn't seem right. I'm glad I didn't know about this yesterday. I would've felt I had to say something to him...and I don't think I would've had the nerve.'

Molly's tension evaporated. It would be easier just to allow her family to believe that Sholto hadn't even considered marriage. They would never understand how she felt. He didn't love her, he didn't need her and he would never have dreamt of asking her to marry him if she

hadn't been pregnant. All Sholto wanted was her child.
And that wasn't enough.

It was after nine when she returned to Templebrooke.
Ogden greeted her with the news that Sholto was no
longer there. Late that afternoon, he had flown out to
Italy.

'Italy?' Molly queried weakly, an intense sense of disappointment filling her.

'A major fire in one of his late father's companies,
madam,' Ogden explained helpfully. 'Suspected arson.
A caretaker and a security guard were injured. I should
think Mr Cristaldi will be away for several days.'

And yet he hadn't left her a personal message or
phoned her even though he'd known where she was. Nor
had he asked her to accompany him. Molly went to bed,
gutted by her own misery. Sholto was angry with her
and she could cope with that when he was around but
not when he was away. Still, at least the fire hadn't taken
place in New York, she found herself thinking. Then she
felt little and mean and selfish for that thought when
innocent people had been hurt.

The following evening, he phoned her from Milan, his
deep, dark drawl cool and polite. 'I'm afraid I don't
know when I'll be back. The police need all the help
they can get.'

'How are the men who were hurt?'

'The security man is in Intensive Care but he's young
and strong and there's a good chance he'll make it...the
old caretaker died.' Sholto's voice roughened tellingly.
'His family's devastated and I'll get the bastard respon-
sible for this if it kills me!'

Travelling back to the town house the next morning,
Molly thought over that conversation and a curious sense
of shame engulfed her. At twenty she had been in awe
of Sholto, had seen the looks, the wealth, the sophisti-

cation...the polished outward image. But how well had she ever got to know the man she loved? she asked herself now.

She had already been shaken by the kindness and tact with which he had handled Nigel and Lena. Somehow he had got down to their level to explain everything in terms they could understand. He had controlled his famous impatience and his intellectual intolerance for stupid questions, and to crown those virtues he had actually admired their home to make them relax and feel more comfortable with him. Her brother's house was a towering monument to very bad taste.

Furthermore, few men of Sholto's standing would devote so much time and attention to the injury of one employee and the death of another. Oh, they might pay lip-service—visit the hospital, speak a few words to the bereaved—but they would stop short of really caring or becoming personally involved because there would always be some other employee available to take charge of that onerous responsibility. But Sholto hadn't gone by that route, hadn't reached for that excuse. And all those actions spoke louder than words. Underneath that surface of cool detachment lurked a male worthy of far more respect than she had been giving him.

Two days later, Sholto rang her to tell her he had just flown in to Heathrow but that he had to head straight into the office because a lot of work had piled up while he had been out of the country. A man had been arrested for arson. He didn't have the time to tell her the whole story, he said. His voice had that distant edge it got when he was already ninety-nine per cent thinking about something else and yet it was the first time he had spoken to her in over twenty-four hours. Molly came off the phone feeling frightened.

Late afternoon, Ogden knocked on the door of the

sitting room where she was reading and announced with an air of deeply approving satisfaction, 'The Reverend Mr Seaton, madam.'

Molly shot out of her armchair with a look of guilty dismay. Donald advanced with a troubled light in his frank eyes.

'I was planning to call and tell you where I was...I *was*!' Molly told him, squirming with embarrassment.

'You would've waited until I came back from New Zealand,' Donald forecast with mortifying accuracy as he took a seat. 'But when Lena chose to confide in me—'

'Lena did *what*?' Molly broke in.

'I don't think she meant to tell me but she was worried about you and the news that you were...er..."in the family way", as she put it, slipped out,' Donald revealed wryly. 'So naturally I felt that I should go and have a word with Sholto...'

Molly cringed. 'You shouldn't have done that, Donald.'

'And I hadn't been with him five minutes before I realised that you had been less than honest with your own family. Sholto asked you to marry him and you turned him down yet you are still living here. I doubt that he will make that offer again, Molly.'

'He doesn't love me...I'm not prepared to marry him just because...well, just because I'm pregnant,' Molly countered in a stifled undertone, never having felt more uncomfortable with Donald in her life.

'That's false pride...and I think you'll lose him completely if you persist with that attitude.'

Molly paled, her stomach clenching.

Donald sighed heavily. 'My reading of Sholto is that when he doesn't gain the result he expects he tells himself that he never wanted it in the first place. He has a much more dangerous temperament than you have, Molly. He doesn't let the anger out, he broods.'

'What did he say?' Molly pressed uneasily.

'He was grimly amused in not the nicest of ways and he kept his own counsel right to the end. He said that marriage would best meet the baby's needs but that if you didn't want it that was fine by him. He was cold, dismissive as he said it...' Donald's brown eyes were perturbed. 'I received the impression that Sholto is extremely bitter, Molly...and if you're saying no to marriage in the hope that he will inundate you with all the reasons why you should say yes I'm afraid you may well be waiting for something that isn't going to happen.'

Sheer cold fear filled Molly because she had always respected Donald's perception. Long after he had gone, she paced the floor. Had she been doing that? Had she been hanging out for persuasion and reassurance? But what entitlement did she have to that hope after some of the things she had said to him that morning? She had thrown his proposal back in his teeth with malicious pleasure, indeed hadn't even allowed him to *make* that proposal.

She had been negative, accusing and martyred and suddenly she was ashamed. She had thought only of her own pride and feelings, not even once about *his*. Donald had known all too well what her bottom line was. And take away the false pride and Molly was now facing that same hard reality. Ultimately, whatever it took, whatever it cost, she could not bear to lose Sholto again.

She was coming down the stairs, dressed for dinner, when Sholto came home. He looked devastatingly handsome and suddenly so precious to her, more precious still when she recognised the lines of strain girding his mouth and the shadowed darkness of his eyes.

He saw her and stilled. 'Have I time to get changed?'

'Of course...' Molly tested a rather nervous smile on him.

'Has Nigel bombed out of his training course already?' Sholto enquired with rich cynicism.

Molly tensed. 'I—'

'There has to be some reason why you should be smiling at me. After all, I am the guy who stands convicted of wrecking your life,' he reminded her very drily.

Discomfiture sent a wave of scarlet climbing up Molly's throat.

Fifteen minutes later Sholto joined her at the dinner table, freshly shaven but casually clad in a pair of faded blue jeans and a sweater. Maybe it was over-sensitive of her but she felt he might be making some sort of statement. She was wearing a green watered silk evening suit, selected with care from the clothes he had bought her.

She fiddled with her cutlery and cleared her throat uncomfortably. 'I've been thinking over your proposal—'

'I don't actually recall proposing,' Sholto inserted with lethal effect.

Shot down in flames, Molly swallowed hard. 'I was very upset...and, well, I may have said some things I didn't really mean.'

'Really?' Sholto said very discouragingly, lounging fluidly back from the table and cradling his wineglass elegantly in one lean brown hand.

'You're not making this easy for me, are you?' Her eyes were full of reproach.

'Give me one good reason why I should.' His shimmering golden gaze rested on her in unashamed challenge. 'We got you pregnant together, Molly. I am no more proof against temptation than the next man. You weren't very receptive to my efforts to clear the air the next morning or when I took the trouble to come and see you a couple of weeks later, hoping that by then you would be more approachable. But all you could focus on was your brother and I couldn't even get a hearing unless I focused on him too.'

His candid condemnation shook her. 'You said some very hurtful things that night at Freddy's,' Molly protested defensively.

'I get upset too but rarely do I say things I don't mean.'

She studied her starter with a shrinking appetite. 'I'm willing to marry you.'

'It has to be *want*,' Sholto told her softly. 'We're unlikely to make one anniversary on *willing*. It's a wishy-washy word and I am not a wishy-washy male, *cara*.'

'All right…I *want* to marry you…do you think you've got your full pound of flesh now?' Molly could not resist asking, for he had made her jump through hoops of fire in punishment for her refusal almost five days earlier.

'Was that what I was doing?' Sholto poured himself another glass of wine and looked reflective. 'If we marry, I don't want any more of that lachrymose sex-is-a-sin nonsense when you enjoy it as much as I do. And if you ever try to get a rise out of me again by giving the come-on to another man I will embarrass you so severely you will never repeat the experiment in this lifetime. Never bring our personal problems into public view.'

Molly had changed colour several times during that pithy lecture, travelling from embarrassment to rage and then back again. 'You stuck me at the far end of the table that night!'

'Naturally I did. I put you beside Natalie who chatters incessantly. It was a business dinner. Believe it or not, you were placed at the foot of the table for your own comfort and enjoyment.'

Molly flushed.

'We'll get married in the private chapel at Templebrooke. It's still in occasional use. The Press will tear their hair out but they won't get a single photo. Nigel and Lena will act as our witnesses. I'll apply for a special licence. Freddy's kid brother, Ned, is now a bishop and he will both grant the licence and perform the ceremony.'

Molly was breathless. 'You seem to have it all worked out.'

'Wear something bright. Anything even remotely like a wedding dress would rouse unfortunate memories,' Sholto told her flatly.

And then he simply changed the subject. He told her about the man whom the police had arrested for arson in Milan. A disaffected former employee with a history of mental problems, made wretched by the discovery that the fire he had set had extracted a human toll.

'You see, it's most unwise to make snap judgements about people,' Sholto drawled, shrewd dark eyes curiously intent. 'People are rarely what they seem to be. But I must say that Donald was rather predictable in his earnest and sincere need to help us both.'

Molly stiffened. 'I know that...so what are you saying?'

Sholto dealt her a slow, steady smile. 'I fired him up and sent him home to you and it fairly did the trick, didn't it, *cara*?'

As she worked out the ramifications of that amused assurance, Molly's bosom swelled with outrage. 'How dare you use Donald like that?'

'Of course, you would've fallen off your high horse eventually, but it's preferable that we should marry quickly, rather than make it blatantly obvious that we're retying the knot because you're expecting my child,'

Sholto drawled softly. 'I always think that a visibly pregnant bride may risk leaving the uncharitable with the impression that the groom was dragged reluctantly to the altar.'

Lena gaped when she saw Molly's dress. It was scarlet, off-the-shoulder and swirled to a halt four inches above the knee. There was nothing remotely bridal about that flirty hemline.

'You look terrific in it,' her sister-in-law finally conceded. 'Only I would've thought Sholto would've fancied you in something more...well, traditional.'

But Sholto didn't seem to fancy her in *anything* any more, Molly thought with a dismal sinking sensation inside her. Since his return from Italy, he hadn't even entered her bedroom. Was that because she was pregnant and somehow no longer sexually attractive to him? Or because he was still angry with her? He had worked such long hours over the past five days that she had barely seen him but she had had plenty of time to reflect on her own errors of judgement.

She saw now *so* clearly that she should have stayed and talked at Freddy's house and definitely shouldn't have used Nigel's predicament like a battering ram to hold Sholto at a distance and prevent him from getting personal when he'd come to her office. He had seen that as blackmail and he had acted accordingly by calling her bluff.

Throughout Sholto had been telling her that what had happened between *them* was infinitely more important and she had been telling him that he couldn't have a hearing unless he helped her brother. And what had that been but blackmail? she conceded ruefully now. For, much as she loved her brother, Sholto had had every justification in saying that Nigel was not on his conscience.

'You just don't know you're living, Molly.' Lena wandered slowly around the fabulous bedroom, touching polished wood with reverent fingers, pausing to admire with unconcealed wonder. 'How could you ever have walked away from all this? *And* Sholto? He's so fantastically good-looking and charming...and so what if he made a bit of a hash of things the last time?'

'"A bit of a hash?"' Molly repeated with dazed disbelief, her head whipping round.

'Well, it's my bet that cousin of his just threw herself at him...and then you went off the deep end about her on your wedding night. A lot of men couldn't stick that sort of hassle and abuse.' Lena sighed ruefully. 'And if he'd slept with her before it must've been even easier for him to do it again. There she was, waiting with open arms, probably telling him how much she loved and appreciated him. Men can act like spoilt little boys on the rampage when you hurt their egos.'

'Sholto's ego is rock-solid. I can't imagine what it would take to sink him to the level of a naughty schoolboy!' Molly objected tautly, pacing the room restively from end to end.

Lena looked uncomfortable. 'I just don't think you should still be holding that night against him, Molly. Maybe that's what I really wanted to say.'

'I'm not *still* holding it against him!' It shook Molly to hear her quiet, shy sister-in-law talking with such surprisingly cynical authority on the subject of the male sex.

'You want to be sure that this is really a fresh start for you both.'

'He doesn't love me...he loves her,' Molly whispered tightly. 'How much of a fresh start is that?'

'If he loved her, he'd have married her after you broke

up with him. You're just looking for trouble,' Lena said worriedly. 'That's all over and done with now.'

Molly stared sightlessly out of one of the windows, her heart thudding at the base of her dry throat. Was it over and done with? Would it ever *really* be over? Did that kind of frustrated and impossible love ever die? Lena just didn't know what she was talking about. But then Molly had never told anyone what she suspected. A secret which bound Sholto and Pandora together in a relationship that could never be what they wanted it to be...

If Riccardo Cristaldi *had* had an affair with his wife's sister, Meriel, and fathered her only child, it meant that Pandora was Sholto's half-sister. Even if their birth certificates said otherwise, even if nobody could either prove or seriously suspect that truth, Molly knew that Sholto would never have taken advantage of that cover of ignorance to live an incestuous lie.

Nor could she forget his scorching derision in this same room when he had said that her narrow mind could not comprehend that sex was *not* the dominating factor in every relationship between a man and a woman. It was just possible that he had resisted temptation, that he had never actually been physically intimate with Pandora, and that Molly had read too much into the snatch of conversation she had overheard.

Rather than that exchange signalling a continuing affair, might Sholto simply have been trying to calm Pandora down while comforting her with the promise that in spite of his marriage he would always care for her? Mightn't he still genuinely have intended to give his marriage a fair chance? But Pandora had been determined not to let Sholto go without a fight and Molly had been too shattered by what she had learnt to do anything but play right into Pandora's hands.

For wasn't that what she had ultimately done? Ranting and raving, refusing to listen to him, walking out on their marriage. She had walled herself up with her grief and bitterness, taking pride in her own stubborn inflexibility. But Sholto had walked out first and he had been with Pandora all night... So if she was to believe that they hadn't been engaged in a rapturous reunion, what *had* they been doing?

For the first time, an arrow of doubt had entered Molly's mind as to the completeness of Sholto's guilt. For the first time, she wanted and needed to know what had actually happened that night, no matter how bad that truth might make her feel.

It was cold in the old stone chapel in the grounds. Gooseflesh rising on her bare arms, Molly was walking down the short aisle when Sholto turned from the altar to watch her. His brilliant dark eyes widened and then flashed gold, raking over her in a lightning-fast appraisal. His beautifully shaped mouth curved into a deeply appreciative and amused smile.

The simple ceremony was over quickly. Sholto's great-uncle Ned was not at all like his late brother, Freddy. Large and portly, Ned looked most impressive in his ceremonial vestments but he had a relaxed and cheerful manner and he laughed a lot. Molly's concentration was nil. Her heart was beating very fast. Don't romanticise this marriage, she told herself in urgent warning. He's marrying you because of the baby and nothing has really changed.

As they vacated the chapel, Sholto slid fluidly out of his jacket and draped it round Molly's bare shoulders. The silk lining was wonderfully warm from his body heat. She glanced up at him, suddenly shy as she met the dark golden eyes trained on her. 'I'm afraid I didn't think about the temperature when I went shopping.'

'You *look*,' Sholto savoured in a low, sexy growl, 'absolutely delicious.'

Ogden served them with champagne in the drawing room. Molly couldn't take her eyes off Sholto and he couldn't seem to take his eyes off her. Nigel and Lena took their leave while Sholto's great-uncle talked endlessly about Templebrooke's priceless hoard of English and Oriental pottery and porcelain. In the Brooke tradition, Sholto was a collector too. A steady procession of experts from all over the world came by special appointment to view the magnificent display which was housed in four specially adapted rooms in the west wing.

'I shall have to see that reunited pair before I leave,' Ned was saying with determination.

'Of course.' Sholto gave the faintest inclination of his dark head and Ogden crossed the room in response to that silent call to receive instructions. Molly watched the smooth little byplay with amusement.

'How many years have they been apart?' Ned was asking fondly.

'Since the night I was born.' Sholto's lean, strong face was oddly tense.

'I expect you don't even know what we're talking about, my dear.' His great-uncle gave Molly an apologetic smile. 'Sholto's father and my elder brother played a game of poker that same evening. Riccardo was boasting interminably about the most magnificent pair of oviform Kakiemon vases he had recently purchased at vast expense for the Templebrooke collection—'

'Freddy despised him for buying them merely to show that he could afford them,' Sholto inserted. 'My father had no appreciation of the vases as works of art.'

'My crazy brother wagered everything he possessed

against one of the pair,' Ned continued with an incredulous shake of his head. 'And he *won*! Riccardo was appalled and he offered Freddy the most fabulous price in exchange.'

'But Freddy preferred to take the vase home and enjoy it,' Sholto completed in a wry undertone.

Molly blinked. They could not possibly be talking about *her* vase, currently sited on a chest of drawers in her bedroom where *she* could enjoy it. A lean hand curved round her spine to push her gently out to the hall. 'Sholto…' she began with an uncertain frown.

'Of course we all knew that Freddy would give it back to Sholto in his will.' Ned chuckled.

'He didn't,' Sholto murmured in a tone of growing weariness. 'He left it to Molly.'

'Good heavens!' the older man ejaculated in complete amazement. 'He didn't, did he? Old Freddy! Well, fancy that, contrary to the last… Still, it's back in the family now, isn't it?' He laughed even harder and patted Molly's shoulder. 'Quite a dowry you brought with you, young lady. I shouldn't think Sholto would've wanted to fix a value on that particular piece. It has to be priceless.'

Sholto's bold features were rigid, his mouth compressed. He shot the garrulous older man a rueful glance. When they arrived at the biggest display room the central glass tower was already unlocked. Within it, Molly saw the exact mirror image of Freddy's vase. The sight transfixed her. Ogden entered the room, cradling its match with splayed and reverent hands, sweat breaking on his concerned brow as he very, very gently set the second vase into the vacant space beside the other.

'An unforgettable moment!' Ned carolled, slapping Sholto approvingly on the back and demonstrating his complete inability to sense the explosive tension in the atmosphere. 'The crowning event of your wedding day, my boy. A too long awaited reconciliation...a reunion...'

There was a lot more in the same sentimental vein but Molly had gone deaf. Numb with incredulity, she surveyed her vase, her *priceless* vase, with its three pretty panel pictures of Oriental ladies, gentlemen, birds and cherry blossom picked out in coloured enamels. She was still standing there, pale as parchment, when Sholto returned from seeing his ebullient great-uncle out to his vintage Rolls-Royce.

Her pinched profile turned, green eyes awash with shocked condemnation. 'How *could* you not tell me?'

Disturbingly calm dark eyes met hers levelly. 'Had you auctioned off that vase to save your brother's skin, it would have been the most appalling betrayal of Freddy's last wishes.'

CHAPTER NINE

MOLLY flinched from that unapologetic response. She was in total turmoil. 'How much...just how *much* is Freddy's vase worth?'

'As one of a unique pair, infinitely more to me than to anyone else,' Sholto admitted with surprising candour. 'That's why Freddy left it to you. He was convinced that I would approach you to buy it back—'

'I'd never have let you buy it!' Molly interrupted in a sudden eruption of temper. 'I would have smashed it into a thousand pieces before I would've sold it to you!'

'Freddy was very fond of you. He was extremely upset when we split up. For some reason, he was frantically keen to bring us together again,' Sholto murmured very quietly, his cool increasing in direct proportion to her fast shredding control.

'You still haven't told me what that vase is worth!'

Distaste hardened Sholto's darkly handsome features. 'More than half a million on the open market. However, it could fetch considerably more as the only other known example of that date is its partner and it will never be sold.'

'Half a million pounds plus?' Molly whispered in ragged disbelief. 'And you *knew* that I hadn't the slightest suspicion!'

She whirled away from him, fighting a desperate battle to control her flailing emotions. She had actually had the means to help her brother without recourse to either Sholto or his wealth. But Sholto hadn't been prepared to tell her that fact and indeed had relied on her ignorance to persuade her into a devil's bargain. Molly was devastated by that revelation.

'All along you knew...' she mumbled sickly.

'Nigel didn't deserve that big a sacrifice, Molly. At the very least, Freddy hoped that his legacy would give *you* financial security. At best he hoped it would reunite us,' Sholto said in a flat undertone.

'Allow me to decide what my brother deserves!'

Sholto surveyed her with cold exasperation. 'Nigel needs to grow up, stand on his own two feet and accept responsibility. If you'd settled his debts for him, he would have been back in just as much trouble within another two years at most and what would you have done then?'

'You're just trying to justify playing on my ignorance!' Molly slung at him painfully.

'Molly...that vase was delivered to you by a specialist courier in reams of protective packaging. Nine out of ten people would have worked out for themselves that it was an extremely valuable piece.'

'I had too much else on my mind at the time! And how could I ever have dreamt that it was valuable when Freddy lived as he did? Even his house belonged to your family!'

'Freddy had a very comfortable trust fund but his tastes were simple. He took that vase from my father because he was tired of being treated like a stupid, middle-aged old codger by a domineering, arrogant man who bragged constantly about his possessions.' Sholto studied her flushed and furious face and his mouth tightened. 'The vase is yours, Molly. If you wish I will buy it from you—'

'I'd rather break it!' she swore.

In coolly contemptuous challenge, Sholto tossed a key down on the top of the nearest display case. 'Go

ahead...but in ten minutes I will still expect you downstairs. We have to leave for the airport.'

'The airport?' Molly echoed blankly.

'We're flying out to the Caribbean for our honeymoon.'

Molly went rigid, throwing him a look of scornful
disbelief. 'After *this*? You've just got to be kidding!'

Implacable dark eyes struck sparks off her defiant
stare. 'No, *cara*, I am not kidding. And if you're still
here staging a sit-in ten minutes from now I have every
intention of turning you over my knee. You won't sit
down on that luscious derrière for the best part of a
week!'

Face burning with outrage, teeth clenched, Molly arrived in the hall exactly nine and a half minutes later.
In explosive silence, she climbed into the car still wearing her flamboyant red dress because she hadn't given
herself time to change.

As Sholto landed the helicopter on the purpose-built pad
to the north of the villa, the little island of Carvalho Cay
tilted in a dizzy blue of lush green vegetation silhouetted
against a jewelled sea of blue. Not in the mood to be
impressed, Molly climbed out into the balmy warmth of
early evening, feeling cross and crumpled.

She had slept or pretended to sleep for most of the
flight on Sholto's private jet and had then enjoyed a
shower and a meal, if not a change of clothes. She was
so sick of her red dress she was ready to ceremonially
burn it. Smoothly assuring her that he liked her just as
she was, Sholto had flatly refused to have her luggage
brought out of the cargo hold.

The long, low villa had been designed to merge with
the surrounding trees and the setting had all the unspoilt
natural beauty of a forest glade. It was breathtaking. For

hours on end Molly had only spoken to Sholto when she was forced to do so but curiosity finally overpowered her. 'You never mentioned this place before.'

'Four years ago, I planned to surprise you. We were to have flown out here the morning after the wedding.' Sholto stood back for her to precede him into a spacious tiled hall decorated with earthenware urns of fresh white flowers. 'My father bought Carvalho Cay and built this house but my mother never knew of its existence. This was his hideaway.'

'You mean he brought his women here.'

'You do have a special way with words, *cara*. You manage to make it sound quite disgusting.'

'He was a married man,' Molly said uncomfortably.

'My mother gave him me and then opted for a separate bedroom. She considered her duty done.' Sholto's tone was dry. 'He loved her but she only married him because he could afford to restore and maintain Templebrooke. She was a cold woman and he was a very warm-blooded man. I don't blame him for seeking consolation elsewhere. He did try to be discreet.'

Was that an enlightening glimpse of Sholto's morality? An affair was fine as long as it was discreet? Was that why Pandora was now based in New York? Irritably suppressing those frantic inner questions, Molly looked at Sholto. His dark eyes lingered on her with disturbing intensity, a faint half-smile beginning to curve his lips.

Her breath shortened in her throat and she sucked in a deep, steadying lungful of air. 'I want to get changed.'

'Are you hungry?'

'Not at all.'

In what she took for silent acquiescence, he led her upstairs and pressed open a carved door on a bedroom that was the last word in luxury. Molly crossed the floor to get a better look at the view through the sliding glass doors. She was utterly enchanted by the waterfall and the spacious natural pool she saw beyond. No wonder his father had chosen this particular site on which to build. As she stood there, she unzipped her dress and stepped out of it with a sigh of relief.

'*Dio*...I wondered what you were wearing underneath,' Sholto murmured thickly. 'Turn round.'

Molly jerked round, not in obedience but in shock. Having heard the door close, she had assumed she was alone and that he was safely on the other side of it. But, lounging back against that same door, Sholto was absorbing the full effect of the scarlet satin and lace corselette lovingly cupping the voluptuous swell of her breasts and shaping her still tiny waist.

'*Per l'amor di Dio*...' he groaned as his gaze moved down to survey the diminutive cobweb grey silk panties that toned with the sleek lace-topped stockings that encased her slim, shapely legs. 'If I'd known what you were concealing, I would've ravished you while we were still airborne.'

Her cheeks a hot rose-pink, Molly fought a craven prompting to haul on the dress again while fiercely regretting her impulsive urge to splash out on fancy lingerie and surprise him. 'I'm still very angry about that vase business!' she warned him in a furiously defensive rush. 'And I'm not spending the night with you! Do you hear me?'

'I hear you but I'm not listening.' Sholto reached behind him and depressed the lock on the door. 'I'm looking at an erotic fantasy in the flesh. It would take physical force to remove me from this bedroom. In any case, even if I wasn't burning up with sheer unadulterated lust and the effects of nearly two weeks of cold showers, you've forgotten one little thing.'

'One little thing...?' Molly repeated unsteadily, striving not to be entrapped by the compelling sexual fire in those smouldering golden eyes centred on her.

'I really can't be expected to relax until we have consummated this marriage...not after our last unfortunate experience,' Sholto pointed out with lazy mockery. 'An annulment is not exactly what the average red-blooded bridegroom longs to see emblazoned in newsprint.'

'How about "SHOLTO DITCHES FRIGID BRIDE"?' Molly could not resist stabbing back. 'Do you think I longed to see that?'

'How about being asked by a sneering, weasel-faced paparazzo why I failed to get my bride horizontal?' Sholto traded, his vibrantly handsome features clenching hard and darkening at that offensive recollection. 'And, believe me, not one of them phrased it that politely. They were considerably more crude, *cara*.'

Molly flinched and bridled. How dared he throw that humiliating information in her face? How dared he tell her that disgusting, horrible men had been referring to her in such terms?

'Considering that during the whole of our engagement you had about as much interest in getting me horizontal as a celibate monk might have had, I am truly amazed that you should've considered yourself mortally offended by such questions!' Molly shot back at him in sudden driven retaliation.

She had the rare satisfaction of seeing Sholto look utterly stunned.

'A celibate monk...?' Incredulous dark golden eyes landed on her like laser beams striking a target.

'With your reputation I thought you'd be expecting me to sleep with you the first week but I soon learnt my mistake, didn't I? I might as well have been dating a eunuch. You didn't make one serious pass at me!' Molly practically spat at him, remembered pain assailing her at the memory of how inadequate she had felt as a woman after they had finally parted. 'And now, for some crazy, perverse reason, you've changed your mind about me.'

'A eunuch,' Sholto intoned with difficulty. 'Correct me if I'm wrong but are you or are you not the shrinking virgin who leapt a foot in the air if I so much as laid a hand on your breast?'

Molly coloured hotly and squirmed. 'I wasn't shrinking, I was just shy…'

'When I think of how hellish hard I found it to control myself and listen to you talking now, I wonder what planet I'm on,' Sholto breathed with sudden rawness. 'You had more inhibitions than a hedgehog has spines…and an even more major drawback.'

He had found it hard to control himself around her *then*?

'Drawback?' she queried unevenly.

'Your stepfather sat up waiting for you to come home every time you went out with me. And one night you left your jacket behind in the car and I drove back minutes later to return it,' Sholto revealed grimly. 'I stood outside the front window and listened to that sadistic old buzzard lecturing you about promiscuity and telling you he'd throw you out of the house if he even once had cause to suspect that you were sleeping with me!'

A stricken gasp had escaped Molly during that confession. Suddenly she wanted to curl up and die with humiliation. At the time, those warning harangues and threats had put her through a nightmare of mortification. She had dreaded going home to face her stepfather's coldly suspicious eyes and his demeaning demand that she account for every hour she had spent in Sholto's company.

Sholto vented a harsh, humourless laugh. 'He was

talking to you as if you were a raving nymphomaniac on the loose. No longer did I need to wonder why you were the way you were. I learnt everything I needed to know listening to that bastard bully and humiliate you. *Dio*…I really don't know how I kept my fist out of his smug, self-satisfied face after that!'

Molly bent her head, her fair skin burning. 'I had no idea…' The admission was stifled. 'I'd have died a thousand deaths if I'd known you'd heard him talking to me like that.'

'If I had made love to you then, you'd have slunk guiltily back into that house like a fallen woman and your stepfather would've guessed exactly what you had been doing,' Sholto forecast ruefully. 'I didn't want to put you through that. I knew you weren't capable of lying to him. You'd have confessed and he'd have made you feel like a whore.'

As she finally understood what had lain behind his astonishing restraint all those years ago, Molly just wanted the floor to open up fast and swallow her before she had to meet his eyes again. 'Probably…'

'You used to look at me with the most incredibly arousing combination of hunger and curiosity.' Sholto expelled his breath in a slow hiss. 'For the first time in my life, I was prepared to wait for gratification. But the biggest joke of all has to be that once I adjusted to that novel concept I found anticipation gave me a quite seriously erotic buzz.'

All Molly could think about was the disastrous conclusion that had been his ultimate reward. 'I didn't realise… I'm sorry I said what I did,' she muttered shakily.

'A monk…a eunuch,' Sholto gritted with sudden savage amusement. 'That was the longest period of celibacy I had had since I was fifteen.'

Sholto being noble and unselfish. Molly studied the

carpet. How could she ever have guessed when he concealed so much from her?

'Do you think you could explain again why you didn't tell me that Freddy had left me something more than a little keepsake? And maybe I would understand better this time,' she proffered with new generosity as his feet appeared in her line of vision.

Sholto bent down and gently untwisted her tightly linked hands, separating them, and she clenched them instead by her sides. He crouched down fluidly on one knee and looked up at her, his eyes scorching slivers of brilliance below dense black lashes. 'All the reasons I quoted plus one very obvious one...or don't you recall me telling you that when I want something I go all out to get it?' he murmured teasingly as he reached up and snapped loose a suspender.

'What are you doing?' Molly gasped.

'What do you think?' Sholto enquired huskily, snapping loose the next and rolling down a stocking with slow, caressing hands to slide it off her foot. 'I fully appreciate how much nerve it must have taken for you to go into a shop and buy lingerie like this. But you steeled yourself and did it for *me*...'

At that tenderly amused purr of satisfaction, Molly turned as hot as her corselette in colour. 'I *couldn't* wear anything normal with that dress.'

'So you broke out into scarlet and suspenders... Stop trying to spoil my pleasure in the first clear invitation you have ever given me.' Sholto smoothed the second stocking down a now trembling slender thigh. 'You have the most beautiful skin...'

'Have I?' Her voice emerged high and breathless enough to startle her. Her heart was going thumpety-thumpety-thump in concert with her struggling lungs.

'The most glorious hourglass shape.'

'People think I should be a bit thinner,' Molly mumbled.

'*Never!*' Sholto said with impressive conviction, skimming reverent hands up over the curvaceously feminine swell of her bottom and making her quiver like a leaf in a high wind.

'Or have one of those breast-reduction ops...' she whispered almost inaudibly.

'Who the hell suggested that?' Sholto demanded wrathfully.

'Can't remember,' she framed breathlessly.

'You have gorgeous breasts...'

She lost the ability to breathe altogether as long fingers hooked into the panties and slowly, gently eased them in a downward direction. She shot her hands down to cover herself in sudden embarrassment. But Sholto buried his mouth in her stomach, catching her defensive hands briefly with his to still the movement, resting there for a second or two while he felt the wild tremors running through her taut length. 'And you have my baby cradled in there,' he said with immense satisfaction.

Molly's legs were shaking so badly, her hands reached down to clutch wildly at his hair and steady herself. With a rueful laugh he bowed his forehead briefly against the quivering, tensing muscles of her stomach and sighed with only faint regret, 'Let's go to bed, *piccola mia*.'

Sliding fluidly upright, he lifted her high in his arms and gave her one passionately hungry kiss before he laid her gently down on the wide divan bed. She felt as if he had stolen her soul with that one kiss. Her green eyes darkened pools of sheer longing and love, she watched him peel off his clothes with the inherent grace that accompanied his every movement. And she thought fiercely then, He's *mine*; he's more mine now than he's ever been hers because I have his baby inside me.

'By the end of three weeks...' Sholto began lazily.

'Three weeks?' she echoed in surprise.

'By the time we go home, I'll have you wandering about this island as naked as a jaybird,' Sholto forecast ambitiously.

'I don't think so,' she warned. 'Maybe just in a sarong or something,' she added after careful thought.

He threw back his darkly handsome head and burst out laughing, lion-gold eyes vibrant with amusement. It felt so good to see him relax to that extent. He strolled across to the bed, gloriously unconcerned by his rampant state of arousal, and he could afford to be, Molly conceded, considering that she couldn't drag her fascinated eyes from that incredibly beautiful and virile sun-bronzed body of his. Deep down inside she was already melting like honey heated to boiling point.

Sholto came down on the bed behind her and curved her back into contact with his warm, hair-roughened chest. 'You must've been tortured wearing this corselette for so many hours,' he murmured with a hint of guilt, but only a hint.

He dealt with the zip, spread the parted edges of the confection apart and let his hands slide up with hungry possessiveness to cup the fullness of her bared breasts. Molly shuddered in response, eyes half-shut as she watched his knowing brown fingers delicately circle the poutingly erect tips and play on their extreme sensitivity until her head fell back against his shoulder and she was moaning under the shocking intensity of that pleasure, watching abandoned for the greater excitement of simply feeling what he was doing to her shivering, ultra-responsive body.

He brought her round to him when she was just a mass of quivering nerve-endings and she grabbed at him with wild hands to hold him close and kiss him with all the breath left in her body. Wanting, aching, needing more strongly than ever before.

Sholto drew back with a ragged laugh of surprise from the assault. Then he slowly knotted his hand into her madly tumbled hair and looked down into her eyes. 'That was no one-night stand at Freddy's house,' he said softly, dark golden eyes sweeping her suddenly anxious face. 'It was unbelievably exciting and I lost control and behaved like a rat afterwards but that doesn't make that night any less special.'

She nodded, throat thickening, vaguely grasping that he was trying to soften her memory of that encounter because that had been the night the baby had been conceived. She buried her face in the satin-smooth hollow of one broad shoulder, snatching in the hot, aroused scent of him as if she couldn't live without it.

He ran a hand up the extended length of her inner thigh, making every tiny muscle twitch, and then he turned her face back up, holding her still while he kissed with his fingers splayed over her cheekbone. The hot excitement took over again as he explored her with gentle, tormenting fingers, discovering how wantonly moist and ready and unbearably aroused she already was.

He spread her beneath him with a sudden growl of very male hunger but he entered her so slowly, she almost died in the seconds that seemed to her frustrated body to last for ever. She tilted her hips, curved her thighs around him in an invitation as instinctive and old as time itself. He groaned and suddenly surged deep inside her with breathtaking force. She cried out at the height of that hot liquid pleasure and then was lost, utterly abandoned and lost to everything but his driving sexual domination.

'You're learning too fast how to push me over the edge,' Sholto sighed languorously in the aftermath of their third bout of lovemaking, folded round her like a sunbathing big cat, content with satiation. 'But you've had it with non-consummation now and you have no hope whatsoever of catching me on a charge of adultery. I wouldn't have the energy.'

Molly flinched as if he had slapped her and before she could catch the words back she had opened her mouth and said painfully, 'But you did the last time!'

Sholto thrust her away from him with positive violence and sat up.

Molly shut her eyes tightly, cursing her lack of concentration, her impulsive tongue and the ruin of a wedding night that had so far been like a dream come true.

'You really do pick your moments,' Sholto gritted with clear, cold anger as he sprang off the bed.

A giant lump ached in her throat. 'Sholto—'

'Pandora took an overdose of pills that night,' Sholto bit out with driven reluctance. 'She phoned me to tell me what she was going to do and I thought she was crying wolf but I couldn't afford to rely on that hope. I couldn't ask anyone else to check up on her either. I had no bloody choice and I am not apologising for that night because she'd be dead if I hadn't gone over there!'

Every scrap of colour had vanished from Molly's face. She pulled herself up in the bed, wide eyes pools of horror, her stomach churning sickly. Afraid she could not control her expression, she looked away.

'I smuggled her out through the back entrance of her apartment to a private clinic where she received medical attention. I didn't want the Press to get hold of it. I stayed at the clinic until I knew she was going to be OK and then I went back to her apartment. She had trashed it. I had to tidy it up before her maid arrived and then write a note saying that she would be staying with friends for a few days.'

'Dear God...why didn't you tell me?' Molly mumbled strickenly.

'*Porca miseria*...if you had a clear recollection of what you were like that night you wouldn't be asking me that question and I didn't have the time to reason with you *and* get to her!'

Molly gulped, feeling utterly sick with guilt. 'She must have been in a terrible state to do something like that.'

'She was very upset...about something private,' Sholto conceded grudgingly, the aggressive force in his dark drawl replaced now by a tone of taut constraint.

She knew he wasn't going to tell her any more. But she could fill in the rest for herself and seeing that picture now was like having her heart ripped out of her body while she was still alive. It filled her with unbearable pain. He must have had a huge burden of guilt to bear. He had not had the ability to be in two places at once. Pandora had gone home alone and in distress. He must have felt torn in two. Molly had taken refuge first behind a locked bedroom door and then, when he had smashed the lock, had flown into the bathroom instead, only emerging when silence had fallen to find him waiting for her. And only minutes after that Pandora had called.

'You should have at least *told* me what she had said on the phone,' Molly reasoned unevenly, recalling her own ranting and raving histrionics. 'It wasn't fair not to tell me.'

'Wasn't it? When you had already made it brutally clear how much you hated her?' Sholto pushed a weary hand through his hair and spun away from her to extract a pair of blue jeans from a drawer in one of the built-in units. 'I'll never understand why you behaved that way that night and I just couldn't take it seriously... All of a sudden you were accusing me of having an affair with her, screeching that I'd only married you to have children. Had all that been building up inside you...where the hell did all that nonsense come from?'

All of a sudden and with a deep sense of shock Molly registered the drawbacks of hurling sobbed recriminations through solid doors. Sholto hadn't grasped that she had heard him with Pandora that evening. Uncertainly, she turned her head away. Did she want to tell him now? Did she want to dredge all that up when he had still not told her the whole truth? But then very probably he never would and maybe it was safer that way, she conceded painfully. What wasn't put into words might well be easier to live with.

'I have never been sexually intimate with my cousin. Let me say that once,' Sholto breathed with fierce insistence. 'And don't ever ask me to defend myself on that subject again.'

Shaken by that savage candour, Molly met stunning dark eyes that unflinchingly held hers. Much of the tightness in her muscles eased. 'OK.'

'And if Pandora was spiteful to you behind my back I wasn't aware of it. You didn't complain.'

'I didn't want to sound childish.'

Sholto shot back one of the sliding doors. 'I need some fresh air...'

Molly cleared her throat nervously. 'I wasn't staying at the vicarage the day that my stepfather put the police on you...actually I didn't go home for several weeks... I was with Jenna, my best friend. She let me stay with her.' And then, drawing a hurried breath, she told him how Jenna's impulsiveness had led to that newspaper article about Pandora.

Disconcertingly, Sholto shrugged. 'It doesn't matter now. It's all water under the bridge. But if it's any consolation to you that's why I let you go. Pandora didn't need to be kicked when she was already down.'

'Have you the slightest idea what *I* was going through at the same time?' Molly demanded painfully.

'If you had had the smallest atom of trust in me, if you had loved me one ounce as much as you said you did, you would've been waiting for me when I came back at dawn.' Burnished dark eyes challenged her shaken face.

'If you had ever told me that you *had* one ounce of love for *me*, maybe I would have had that trust and maybe I would've been there waiting.' Her voice died away as she saw a dark flush arc up over his bold cheekbones and the sudden screening of his eyes. 'You demand and expect so much more than you are prepared to give, Sholto.'

'Maybe nobody ever gave me that kind of love before...and maybe sometimes it felt good and sometimes it felt suffocating...and you didn't give me the time or the space to respond,' he countered grimly, and strode out into the darkness.

Weak as a kitten, Molly slumped back against the tumbled pillows. A clearing of the air. Why did it have to make her feel so dreadful? Why, when it was far too late, did she have to be experiencing the most appalling sense of guilt and compassion for a woman she had spent so long hating? And how *could* Sholto be so tormentingly cruel as to inform her that he had decided to write off their first marriage only *after* that wretched newspaper had printed that hateful, malicious article about Pandora?

'When you dip even a toe in dirty water, you get soiled,' Donald had told her and Donald had been right. Telling Jenna too much had been Molly's back-door method of stabbing Pandora in the back.

Suffocating? She winced. Insecurity had made her cling and be too possessive in public. It had also made her throw noisy I-want-you-to-feel-guilty scenes as she'd constantly sought a reassurance he apparently could not give her. Indeed, the more desperate she had become, the further and faster Sholto had backed off...just as he was doing *now*!

In a sudden movement, Molly leapt out of bed and stalked over to the sliding doors to throw them both wide on the star-studded night. She pictured Sholto brooding on the beach, feeling as much entrapped by her as by the sea waves lapping the shore. He had signed up for a three-week stint and now he was stuck.

'I hope a shark gets you!' Molly shouted on a surge of boiling temper and the confident near certainty that she ran little risk of being heard. The exercise was a satisfying vent for her turbulent emotions. 'And if a shark doesn't get you I *will* because you've got absolutely no business leaving me alone again on our wedding night!'

Sholto strolled out of the shadows beyond the pool and stilled like a silent predator in the soft pool of light arrowing out of the bedroom. His shirt was hanging open on his hair-roughened brown chest, long, straight legs sheathed in faded tight denim and set slightly apart.

Molly froze. As her face fell by a mile, he smiled with sudden intense amusement and moved closer. 'That was really telling me, Molly. And most refreshing it was too. I don't like it when you sulk and hide your face from me and turn your back. You never used to do that. You used to wade right in and sock it to me. You are the only woman I have ever met who tells me where to get off and who shouts when I don't want to listen,' he confided smoothly. 'It's a curiously attractive quality.'

'Is it?' she whispered, heart still banging like mad

after the onslaught of that dazzling smile. 'I thought it might send you off to the jungles of Indonesia again.'

A winged ebony brow quirked. Intense dark eyes dropped down in speaking appreciation of her unclothed body. 'I have everything that I want right here...less the threatened sarong.'

Only then registering that she was posing before him as bare as the day she had been born, Molly uttered an only semi-muffled swear word which she had never used in her life before and pelted back to the cover of the bed at speed.

Sholto vented a husky laugh and strolled over to the bed with the indolent cool of a predator prowling on home territory. From the smouldering burn of his dark eyes to the passionate curve of his wilful mouth, he emanated an intense sensuality which mesmerised her.

'I'm glad you feel lonely after a whole ten minutes on your own...it gives me a very good excuse to get back into bed with you,' he imparted, coming down gracefully beside her and peeling off his shirt in one shockingly sexy movement.

CHAPTER TEN

'CHRISTABEL if it's a girl, Jasper if it's a boy. We have a tradition of unusual names in my family,' Sholto informed Molly.

'It's a wonder you settled for marrying a plain ordinary Mary known as Molly.' She hugged her knees as she perched on the concealed ledge in the pool, enjoying the silk-soft ripple of the warm water caressing her skin and the shaded warmth of the sun on her bare back.

Sholto streaked across the pool underwater and surfaced a foot in front of her. 'But you were christened Mary *Ermentrude*.' He laughed as she visibly cringed from the unwelcome reminder. 'A good solid name, that, but not in common use.'

Molly slid her knees down below the water at the exact same moment as he reached for her. He lifted her into his arms, cupping her hips to lock her thighs round his narrow waist. Her heartbeat hit the Richter scale as she collided with glittering dark eyes ablaze with sensual intent.

'You were just sitting there waiting for me to do this...' Sholto registered.

'Is that a complaint?'

'A rousing vote of approval,' he purred in appreciative rebuttal as he waded out of the pool.

Molly dropped her head and let her teeth graze tenderly over the smooth, wet skin of his shoulder and then even more self-indulgently went into reverse over the same path with the soft, nipping pressure of her mouth.

'Mrs Cristaldi...you're exciting the hell out of me.'

'I like doing that...' Indeed Molly was astonished by how much more confident and uninhibited she had felt since she had had the assurance that he had never slept with Pandora and therefore could not possibly be comparing her in any way in that field. So Pandora was still enshrined in his heart—well, it wasn't perfect but she could live with that...couldn't she? Troubled by that thought, she closed it out.

'Three weeks in paradise...we should both be climbing the walls with boredom but I don't want it to end,' Sholto confided almost roughly.

They were flying home that evening and she didn't really want that reminder. She hugged him close in a fierce surge of affection and knew that the sunlight dancing blindingly on the water was dull in comparison to the blinding, wondering happiness that had consumed her with every passing day on Carvalho Cay.

'You will be a wonderful mother, *cara*. Hugs for cut knees, beaming smiles for achievements and buckets of sympathy for disappointments,' Sholto recited as he brought her down on the bed. 'And you'll never lose your naivety because you look at things and always innocently assume that they must be what they appear to be.'

'If that is yet another crack about the fact that I thought the waterfall and the pool were natural features—'

'*And* you argued with me until I pointed out that few ponds rejoice in a complete lack of plantlife and fish and a remarkably convenient set of ledges and steps, not to mention a shallow end, a deep end and a state-of-the-art infiltration system,' Sholto cut in softly.

He had split his sides with laughter when he'd realised that she had been fooled.

'Well, I still think most people would've been taken

in...' Her voice trailed away due to severe shortage of oxygen as she connected with his blazingly intent golden eyes.

He kissed her and her heart went crazy. She held him tight, smoothing loving hands over every part of him she could reach, raw excitement quivering through her in answer as he shifted with a hungry growl and let his tongue stab deep between her eagerly parted lips...

An hour and a half later, she walked out of the bathroom still towelling herself dry. 'Three weeks in paradise,' she reflected with a sunny smile. Not a bad masculine rating for a honeymoon. They had island-hopped in the helicopter when they'd felt like a change of scene. Dominica was only two miles away. They had gone fishing, swum, sunbathed, eaten long, leisurely meals followed by long, leisurely lovemaking. They had also skipped meals to make frantic passionate love and then talk long into the night.

She had learnt so much about his childhood and had done her best to conceal her chilled shudders. As a little boy he had been punished for crying as automatically as he had been punished for shouting or losing his temper, every natural impulse roundly squashed and driven underground because anything less than complete self-discipline had been unacceptable. He'd had an absentee, philandering father and a mother who had pushed him away with a frown of irritation whenever he tried to touch her.

And slowly but surely Molly had begun to understand Sholto as she had never understood him before. He was a very physical male and he had learnt only to express his feelings through physical channels. He communicated first with sex. He could be astonishingly tender, gentle and caring but there had to be that initial physical intimacy before Sholto would let himself go and trust enough to talk. No wonder she had been so shattered by his raw and candid verbal assault on her at Freddy's house! Having established that all-important link, Sholto had shed his reserve and shown his real emotions to her for the very first time.

And that process had just speeded up on Carvalho Cay. As Sholto had let his guard down, she had found that the teasing and the warmth came now without any sexual prompting because he had relaxed with her. His aloof detachment had vanished as if it had never been. It was just a self-defence mechanism... why, oh, why had she never recognised that before?

Only now could she appreciate the simply huge barrier that had dogged their relationship four years ago. She had never had any hope of getting close to Sholto without that initial intimacy. The strength of her love had drawn him as surely as a stack of gold ingots but, new to that experience and uneasy with his own hunger for that all-consuming attention, he had, at times, been repelled by it as well. He had been able to hang onto his reserve then, mask his emotions, walk away without feeling too much pull back. But she didn't think he would find that so easy to do now...

Sholto was working in the computer room. Molly settled down in the cool of the lounge to flick through an English newspaper that was already several days old. She had bought it the day before on Dominica but hadn't got around to reading it. Funny how she had only recently dared to start reading newspapers again. For four years she had shunned them and watched television instead, secure in the knowledge that neither Sholto nor Pandora was likely to appear on the small screen.

The photo of Pandora on the newspaper's gossip page caught her attention first. She then curiously scrutinised the handsome dark male beside her. Her husband-to-be,

Armando, was not a patch on Sholto, she decided. With the feeling that she was coping very well, she then went on to read the accompanying blurb. And instantly all sense of cool was torn from her. After a very public row with Armando in a New York nightclub, Pandora had broken their engagement.

Pandora's marriage was off...Pandora was on the loose again. Molly's stomach gave a sick lurch of fear. How was Sholto likely to react to that news? And how ironic it was that when she was finally ready to talk about Pandora Sholto would swiftly change the subject if she came close, his unease and reluctance patent. *Everything* about Pandora seemed to be highly confidential and private, Molly reflected painfully.

For three weeks, she had been telling herself that whatever had been between them was at an end. But at the back of her mind she never forgot for one moment that the man she loved was not in love with her. Oh, he was fiercely attracted to her, entertained by her company and was quite touchingly ready to adore their baby even before it was born...but he still loved another woman far more than he would ever love her.

'What is the matter with you?' Sholto demanded an hour before the jet came in to land in London.

'I'm just a bit tired, that's all,' Molly muttered, flipping frantically through another magazine, not wanting to meet his eyes, feeling treacherous because she hadn't told him what he so clearly did not yet know. But then she hadn't given him the chance to see that newspaper. In the most ridiculous panic, she had hidden it in one of her suitcases.

'So you don't talk, you don't eat, you just sit there like a wet weekend?'

She was such a coward. *Obviously* he would find out.

Wouldn't it be more normal for her simply to mention it…casually? Then she would be on the spot to see how he reacted. But did she really want to see how he reacted? Could she handle that?

'Molly…?' Sholto prompted impatiently.

She thrust the magazine aside and looked up. 'Pandora has broken off her engagement… I read about it in a newspaper yesterday.'

Sholto paled. Right there in front of her he paled, cheekbones tensing, mouth compressing, dense dark eyes swiftly concealed by the thick curtain of his outrageously long lashes.

The silence lay there and she willed him to break it, say something, *anything*.

The silence continued.

'I'll be in New York next week…I'll see her then,' Sholto drawled with an abstracted frown.

Suddenly she wished he had let the silence last for ever. She surveyed him with great wounded eyes and then her chin came up, her gaze hardening. 'I don't think you should feed an obsession; I think you should starve it.'

'And what's that supposed to mean?'

Her breath rattled in her dry throat. 'I *know* how you feel about her. Surely it's better that you stay away from her…?'

'How I *feel* about her? What the hell are you trying to say?' Sholto demanded.

She had gone too far to back off, Molly registered. She curled her hands together tightly on her lap and, taking a deep breath, related to him exactly what she had overheard pass between him and his cousin on that day four years earlier. He stiffened, sudden comprehension striking him. 'So *that's* why you were behaving like a madwoman that night…that's where all those nonsensical accusations came from…'

Molly blinked in disconcertion, that not having been the response she had expected to receive to her revelation, but, having forced herself to that point, she was now utterly determined to get everything off her chest. 'It was so obvious that you were absolutely crazy about her—'

'Was it really?' Sholto cut in very drily, steadily hardening dark eyes narrowing on her.

Molly averted her gaze. Naturally he would try to reinterpret that little piece of dialogue and attempt to make his side of it, at least, sound more acceptable. 'It was a long time before I finally worked out what was going on between the two of you…because I couldn't understand why you hadn't just got together…if you felt like that about each other,' she persisted, with longer and longer hesitations between her words.

'Yes, a sane and normal mind would boggle,' Sholto agreed with sardonic softness. 'After all, if I wanted Pandora, what was I doing marrying you?'

Molly's hands twisted together. 'It only made sense when I worked out that…well, that you couldn't marry her…couldn't be with her the way you wanted to be,' she muttered, her voice sinking lower and lower as she struggled to work herself up to the very crux of an extremely sensitive subject and to do so with understanding rather than condemnation.

'I'm afraid you are not making any sense at all to me,' Sholto delivered very drily.

'If you were related to each other more closely than other people knew,' Molly practically whispered.

'What are you trying to say?' Sholto sounded incredibly convincing in his impatient demand for her to clarify herself.

'If your father and her mother had had an affair, it would make Pandora your half-sister…'

Silence stretched. Barely breathing, Molly looked up. Sholto was staring at her with an arrested look of sheer incredulous disbelief, his reaction so intense, Molly grasped instantaneously that she had got it wrong, indeed that her suspicions as to his true relationship with Pandora were so wildly offbeam that he could barely absorb the concept of them.

'You think that my father…and *her* mother…*Madre di Dio!*' Sholto vented with such explosive suddenness and fury that Molly jerked in shock and turned pale.

He leapt upright, strode down the aisle between the seats and then swung back as if he couldn't contain himself. His dark features were a mask of pure rage. 'What a thoroughly nasty and dirty mind you have!' he condemned in a blistering attack of outraged derision. 'You sit there and not only do you dare to accuse my father of sleeping with my mother's sister and fathering her daughter, but you also then go on to insinuate that I have formed some unnatural attachment to a woman I know to be my half-sister!'

White as a ghost, shrinking away from his appalled reaction and very much wishing she had kept her mouth shut, Molly studied him with stricken eyes. A sense of horrified humiliation was beginning to engulf her as the manner in which Sholto had framed her beliefs did indeed make them sound grotesquely far-fetched. Indeed at that moment Molly was finding it very difficult to comprehend how she had first begun to develop and believe in such an offensive scenario to explain what she could not understand. 'I'm sorry,' she mumbled almost inaudibly.

'*Dio*…you deserve to be shaken until your teeth rattle in your stupid little head!' Sholto told her roundly, with no diminution in his wrath. 'I have never been so disgusted in all my life. Pandora is indeed the closest thing I have ever had to a sister and I am very fond of her but my father did not have an affair with her mother and there are no grounds whatsoever for anyone to even suggest that he did. He would never have dreamt of starting an affair within his own family circle and I doubt if he saw Pandora's mother more than a handful of times after her marriage because he couldn't stand her husband!'

Molly had turned a bright pink under his contemptuous gaze but she was endeavouring to find some form of self-defence. 'I heard all the gossip about Pandora's father committing suicide,' she muttered frantically. 'People suggesting that you and Pandora might really be brother and sister and that he had found out and—'

At that reference, Sholto's angry face clenched hard and chilled. 'Believe me, that is not why Parker shot himself.'

Molly gathered her shredded dignity, mustered her turbulent thoughts into order and murmured with pleading unsteadiness, 'All right, I made some...some very ill-judged assumptions and I apologise for that but *please* just explain to me why Pandora was so upset and why she was saying the kinds of things she was saying that day if there had never been that sort of relationship between you...'

A flash of complete exasperation appeared in Sholto's eyes and then his gaze veiled, his strong features bleak. 'Without her permission that's not my story to tell. No further explanations *should* be necessary. It should be sufficient for you to know that you grossly misinterpreted what you overheard and that there was never anything between us which threatened you.'

The gulf of silence stretched.

Sholto threw himself back down into a seat across the

aisle, almost as if he couldn't bring himself to return to his former seat opposite her. There was a look of brooding bitterness in his eyes she had never seen before as he studied her and that look shook Molly inside out. 'Sholto…' she began fearfully, terrified of the huge rift which she had suddenly opened up between them in her refusal to leave the past where it belonged.

'But perhaps it's time I told you another story,' he continued flatly, his mouth twisting. 'I met a very attractive girl in a country lane four and a half years ago…and she was quite unlike any other girl I had met. She was very frank and open and warm and she never, ever pretended to be something she wasn't. I fell head over heels in love with that girl…'

Molly jerked, losing colour.

'And I call her a girl because she wasn't a woman. In many ways she was still very immature. Even though she didn't live in a happy home, she still stayed there and never dared to argue against any of her stepfather's unreasonable demands. In short, she was still very unsure of herself as an adult. But I thought I could handle that until she came in contact with my very different lifestyle and quite suddenly began to change…'

Molly bit her lip at the painful accuracy of the picture he drew.

'I wanted to put the wedding back, give us both more time, but I doubted my ability to persuade you that that was not a rejection. The Press would've had a field day with a cancellation, you would've felt humiliated and our relationship would not have survived the stress. I didn't want to lose you, so we soldiered on, not very successfully, and at the first challenge we fell apart…and by the way, Molly, whether you like to admit it or not, you *were* high as a kite on too much champagne that day.'

Colour drenched her strained cheekbones. Her eyes slewed from his but she gave a jerky little nod and compressed her lips, feeling the tears threatening.

'At the same time, a problem I hadn't seen developing suddenly created a major crisis on what should've been a wonderful day. Everything went wrong so fast, my head spun,' Sholto breathed grimly. 'But I did try to sort it out, I did *try* to see you, and all I got was a petition for divorce on the grounds of adultery served on me. That and that article on Pandora marked the bitter end.'

'You never told me you loved me,' Molly whispered chokily, shaking her head as if she could rein back the tears by doing so.

'Maybe I didn't have the words but I thought I showed it…I probably showed it most strongly when you rolled up at the altar looking like Peter Pan in drag,' he completed ruefully.

'I needed you to tell me that you loved me…I needed that reassurance to feel more secure,' Molly framed unevenly.

But Sholto was looking through her as if he couldn't quite see her any more. He expelled his breath in a driven hiss. 'I think you should go down to Templebrooke for a few days…give us both some breathing space. Right now, I am not in the mood to reassure you.'

Molly had gone pale, eyes widening in dismay. 'Sholto, I—'

'*Dio mio*…you drag up the past as if we're still living it! You wouldn't give five minutes of your time four years ago to discuss our marriage and save it…but you're throwing it all up at me now,' Sholto condemned with chilling bite. 'I thought we were happy and at this moment I feel so angry and bitter that I don't trust myself around you.'

'Sholto...' Molly said painfully. 'I love you.'

He cast her an embittered look of derision. 'No, you don't,' he countered with a shocking degree of dismissal. 'You don't know the first thing about love. If you really loved me, you'd expect the odd imperfection and the occasional secret and you wouldn't still be sitting in judgement; you'd *trust* me!'

'I do trust you,' Molly began feverishly.

But Sholto wasn't listening. Studying her with stonily hard dark eyes, he demanded grimly, 'And who was it who continually went out on a limb to get us back together again? It certainly wasn't you! You didn't even have the guts to admit you still *wanted* me...I had to use your brother to get you back and then I had to rely on your pregnancy to keep you with me! And you think *you* need more reassurance, Molly? I think you've already had far more than your fair share!'

Flattened by that hail of recriminations and tears by then overflowing to track down her cheeks, Molly leapt out of her seat and headed for the washroom. When she emerged again ten minutes later, Sholto was on the phone arranging for separate transport for them both, so that they could part as soon as the jet landed.

'I don't want to go to Templebrooke without you,' she whispered tightly, seriously out of her depth with the way that Sholto was behaving now. A little crack had suddenly stretched and burst into a massive rift and she wasn't quite sure yet how it had happened but one thing she was painfully aware of...Sholto was anything but satisfied with her and their relationship.

'I am not about to apologise for needing a little time to simmer down,' Sholto informed her coldly.

And that was that.

CHAPTER ELEVEN

OUTSIDE the airport terminal building, Molly climbed like a sleepwalker into the limousine waiting for her. Donald had warned her that Sholto was very bitter but Molly had not seen that bitterness until it was too late. She hadn't seen it, she conceded, because, unlike her, Sholto had been able to put the past behind him and start entirely afresh on their second marriage.

But that had been rather easier for him since he had never been in her position, had never known what it was to believe that *she* loved someone else. How could he understand how that fearful insecurity about Pandora had haunted her even in the midst of her genuine happiness and contentment?

Yet what had she done today but wreck that happiness? She had deeply offended him with wildly erroneous and unpleasant allegations, the recollection of which still made her cringe and want to die a thousand deaths. And once she had roused Sholto's anger the whole situation had suddenly exploded into something far more damaging and something she could no longer control.

Since Sholto had very obviously never been in love with Pandora and indeed clearly judged himself to be the injured party of their first marriage, he would have had to have quite inexhaustible patience to tolerate Pandora being raised as a bone of contention between them yet again. And Molly knew that Sholto had many virtues but inexhaustible patience was certainly not one of them.

He had brushed off her assurance that she loved him with complete derision and that had really hurt her. Yet before that he had made her ache with pain by finally telling her how much he had loved her four years ago. Even more aware than she had been that their relationship was in trouble, he had still married her rather than risk losing her. For a male as shrewd, coolly logical and practical as Sholto that had been a *very* telling choice.

And what about his accusation that she had already had far more reassurance than she deserved this time around? Right into early evening at Templebrooke, Molly paced the floor of the drawing room, disturbed by the maddening manner in which Sholto could, with a few annoyingly well-chosen words, turn her view of their relationship entirely upside down. For in scornfully describing how *he* had had to make all the major moves which had led to their remarriage he had told her so much.

In her efforts to protect herself and in her conviction that he loved another woman, she *had* fought him every step of the way. He was angry and bitter because he had felt forced to use first Nigel and then their coming child as pressure first to bring her back into his life and, second, to keep her there. And what did that tell her? Sholto had wanted and hoped for far more from her than a willingness to share his bed…bingo, Molly!

Racing over to the phone like a drowning swimmer who had suddenly been thrown a lifebelt, Molly punched out the phone number of the town house. Ogden answered.

'I'm afraid Mr Cristaldi's out, madam.'

'He's still at the office, then,' Molly assumed.

'No, he went out to dine with Miss Stevenson—'

'What?' Molly interrupted, stiffening in shock.

'Miss Pandora, madam,' Ogden clarified, in his in-

nocence evidently thinking that she might not have recognised that surname. 'Would you like the number of
the restaurant or would you prefer to leave a message?'

'Neither...thank you.' Molly replaced the receiver
again.

So Pandora was already back in London. No doubt
she'd headed straight for Sholto like a homing pigeon—
as she always did in times of trouble. That was a recognised pattern of Pandora's, Molly conceded thoughtfully.
And why was it part of the beautiful blonde's pattern?
Because Pandora loved *him*. 'A problem I hadn't seen
developing suddenly created a major crisis,' Sholto had
said of their first wedding day. Had that problem been
his belated realisation that his cousin cherished far from
platonic feelings for him? And did he feel that admitting
that Pandora had loved him or indeed still loved him
would be too much of a betrayal of the other woman?
Was that why he hadn't just told her the truth?

She heard a car raking up the gravel beyond the tall
windows and wandered abstractedly over to see who it
was. It was Sholto's black Ferrari. Her heart hammered
with sudden intense relief as Sholto emerged and then
sank in horror all the way down to her toes as a shining
blonde head and a pair of long, gorgeous legs appeared
out of the passenger side...Pandora!

It took Molly precisely one split second to back away
from the window before she could be seen. They were
supposed to be out eating somewhere together. Why on
earth had he brought Pandora here with him instead? A
frown of bewilderment and frank dismay on her face,
she heard the harried tap-tap of the housekeeper's shoes
across the hall as the bell shrilled and shrilled with savage impatience. Sholto had run into the barrier of the
bolts and chains which were drawn once the daily staff
went home at five. There was a mutter of voices and

then the drawing-room door opened abruptly and Pandora stood framed on the threshold.

The blonde dealt Molly an uneasy, strained look and then glanced over her shoulder at Sholto. 'Oh, do go away and leave us alone,' she said almost pleadingly. 'I hereby swear and promise that I will not say a single word to upset your wife.'

Closing the door, Pandora moved deeper into the room and settled herself tautly down in an armchair. 'I don't know where to begin...' she confessed. 'But then I've never been that great at acknowledging my mistakes and saying sorry.'

'Why do you feel you have to say sorry?' Molly asked uncomfortably.

Pandora grimaced. 'Because I was a real bitch the whole time you were engaged to Sholto and I knew you were outside that door that day and I didn't warn him then or even tell him later,' she admitted ruefully. 'I wanted you to think that he only married you because you could give him kids... I hated you and I wanted to spoil things for you any way that I could.'

'You were successful,' Molly conceded.

Pandora winced but her troubled gaze held steady. 'I'm not the same person I was in those days. I was all mixed up and terribly unhappy and I'm not like that any more,' she stated with quiet confidence. 'Sholto was a major part of my life then. I was very dependent on him and when he got engaged to you I started to panic and feel threatened...'

'You were in love with him,' Molly said with wry sympathy.

'No...not in the sense that you mean.' Pandora stood up again to walk over to the window, her restive tension unconcealed. 'Sholto should've told you everything and then you might have understood. My problems back then all stemmed from a rather gruesome childhood.' She glanced back at Molly, blue eyes pained but steady. 'My father was a violent man. He battered my mother and when she cheated him of that outlet by dying from a heart attack he used his fists on me instead.'

'Oh, no...' Molly mumbled in sick disconcertion.

'He kept me away from school if he marked me too obviously. Often I had to lie and pretend I'd had an accident. Our housekeeper knew what he was doing but she valued her job and just pretended it wasn't happening...and in any case I was ashamed of it,' Pandora admitted starkly. 'I was the golden girl everyone thought had everything and I didn't want people to know the truth. In a sense I helped my father to keep on doing that to me.'

'It must have been a nightmare,' Molly murmured with very real sympathy.

'When I was sixteen, Sholto called in out of the blue one day to pay us a visit. We hadn't seen him in years. My father was at work. I was at home nursing a couple of broken ribs,' Pandora delineated harshly. 'But Sholto saw the bruises on my arms and he wasn't so easily fooled. He got the whole story out of me and drove straight back to London to tell his father.'

'Thank God for that,' Molly whispered.

Pandora grimaced. 'The same day, Riccardo Cristaldi confronted my father. He told him that he intended to inform the social services and apply for custody of me. My father couldn't face that size of a disgrace...' Her voice wavered tellingly.

'And that's why he shot himself,' Molly inserted in appalled realisation, slowly feeling her way down onto a seat.

'I went to live with the Cristaldis in Rome but three months later Sholto's parents died in that air crash. I was supposed to have counselling and all that sort of thing but I refused,' Pandora revealed ruefully. 'I didn't want to discuss what had happened to me with strangers. I thought I could just put it behind me. And for a long time I believed I had. But every relationship I tried to have with a man went wrong and the only constant in my life was Sholto. I was never jealous of his girlfriends until you came along...and then suddenly he didn't have the same time for me and I got more and more frantic—'

'You really don't need to tell me any more,' Molly interrupted.

'I owe it to Sholto.' Her beautiful face stiffened. 'I wasn't really in love with him, it was just that I was so scared of losing the one man I had ever really cared about and trusted. I got it into my head that that could be the foundation for something more... On your wedding day, I just snapped. I wept all over him and told him how much I loved him. He was devastated. Since he certainly couldn't encourage me, all he could do was assure me that he would always be there for me as a friend. You know what happened the night of your wedding...'

'Yes,' Molly confirmed reluctantly.

'That was the most selfish thing of all that I did. I wanted to make him suffer for not returning my feelings,' Pandora confessed uncomfortably.

An awkward silence fell.

'I'm terribly sorry about that newspaper article,' Molly breathed heavily.

'Forget it,' Pandora advised ruefully. 'I cost you your marriage and you lost me a few friends. But something positive did come out of it—for *me* anyway. Sholto finally managed to persuade me to go for counselling and I haven't looked back since then. I'll always be very fond of him but I have my own life now and I also have

Armando.' A warm smile softened her lips, a warmth Molly had never thought to see on that once coolly beautiful face.

'You do?' Molly questioned helplessly. 'I thought—'

'A silly tiff and me getting cold feet before I finally commit myself.' Pandora laughed, flashing the opulent engagement ring adorning her left hand. 'My dress is being made in London. That's why I'm over here. Are you going to come to our wedding?'

Molly smiled, the last of her tension evaporating. 'Oh, yes…and thank you for the invitation.'

'About the only thing we have in common is Sholto,' the beautiful blonde mused with complete candour. 'But for his sake I'd like us to try to be friends. He's the only family I've got left.'

'I don't see a problem with that now,' Molly murmured gently.

'Great…then it was worth me coming down here to sort things out.' Pandora smiled. 'It also means I get to drive Sholto's Ferrari back to town. I don't think he can have thought of that.'

Sholto walked into the room a few minutes later. Outside the engine of the Ferrari ignited with a loud, almost taunting roar. But neither Molly nor Sholto had eyes or ears for anything but each other.

Sholto looked incredibly anxious, intense dark eyes pinned to her face, his strong face taut. 'Pandora insisted on seeing you personally.'

'That was incredibly kind of her…she's so changed, too,' Molly muttered, looking back at him, trying to read what was going on behind those vibrantly handsome features of his. 'If only I'd known. She's had such an appalling time of it.'

'I really don't want to talk about Pandora any more,'

Sholto breathed tensely. 'And I must've been out of my mind this morning to react the way I did.'

'I did give you quite a shock with my ability to add two and two and come up with a distinctly embarrassing five.'

'Did you mean it when you said you loved me?' Sholto bit out tautly.

'Oh, yes…very much,' Molly assured him cheerfully, knowing that this was not the time to stand on injured pride.

His sizzling tension gave and he reached for her with two possessive hands, snatching her up against him and holding her so tightly she could barely breathe. 'I suppose you've already worked out how much I love you.'

'Well, I could do with hearing it firsthand,' Molly said apologetically.

With an unsteady laugh, Sholto lifted his dark head. 'I was knocked for six when I saw you again at Freddy's…and then I was outraged when I saw that ring on your finger. I didn't know what was happening to me and I didn't enjoy losing control in bed with you…but after you'd gone I read all the letters you ever wrote to Freddy.'

Molly stiffened. 'You did *what*?'

'He left them for me in a file marked "Molly's letters". And up until you arrived I had successfully resisted temptation but you hadn't gone ten minutes before I caved in and started to read them,' Sholto confided shamefacedly. 'And when I realised that you had been as utterly miserably unhappy after we broke up as I had been a sort of process of healing began and I stopped feeling so bitter and began wondering how I could persuade you to give me another chance so that we could try again.'

'And I didn't want to listen,' Molly groaned.

'I knew you wanted me…and I suspected and hoped that there might be more to it than that, *cara*,' Sholto admitted, tactfully removing his eyes from her blushing face.

'There was. I never got over you.'

'Good,' Sholto said squarely. 'But I was really furious that you wouldn't just admit that you wanted me too and then Nigel's problems got involved and muddied the water.'

'I'm sorry about that. He had made the most awful mess and it wasn't your responsibility to—'

'Molly,' Sholto broke in, cupping her cheekbones with two soothing hands, dark eyes guilty, 'when I went down and saw Nigel and Lena, I felt like I had been taking a hatchet to the babes in the wood,' he confided with a sardonic twist of his mouth. 'You did the right thing when you made me listen to you. I would've kept an eye on your brother if we'd stayed married. He would never have got into a fix as bad as that if I'd been around.'

Her eyes filled with tears. 'It's very decent of you to say that.'

'*Dio, cara…*' Sholto groaned, sweeping her up into his arms and carrying her out of the drawing room. 'Don't cry. Don't you know that even if I'd hated your brother, which I most certainly don't, I would've ended up helping him just to make you happy?'

Linking her hands round his neck as he carried her upstairs, she blinked back tears. 'If you love me, why were you so appalled when you first suspected I might be pregnant?'

A winged brow climbed. 'I'm amazed you have to ask me that. You were already bursting at the seams with resentment. Impregnating you with my child outside the bonds of holy matrimony was extremely unlikely to advance my cause with you…in fact, it couldn't have happened at a worse time. I hadn't even had a chance to show you how happy we could be together.'

'Do you still feel like that about the baby?' Molly looked anxious.

'Don't be an idiot,' Sholto told her as they entered his bedroom, and he bestowed her upon his bed as if she was a very precious cargo. 'By the time you had finished shouting at me, calling me a selfish, irresponsible toad and letting me know that I had wrecked your life, I was damned grateful that you *were* pregnant…because I could see that that was the only hold on you I had left!'

'Serves you right,' Molly dared, but she smoothed a loving hand over one high cheekbone as she said it. 'All that talk about being constructive and wanting the baby and never a word about wanting me for my own sake!'

'It's a challenge to be so brave when the woman you love looks suicidal because she's carrying your child,' Sholto spelt out heavily. 'And when you said you couldn't even bear to think of that night at Freddy's it cut me off at the knees because I know I may have hurt your feelings but it wasn't as bad as you made it sound.'

'It was wonderful until you got out of bed,' Molly confided, green eyes filled with love. 'And then you had to ruin it.'

'You weren't the only one who was shaken up by what happened between us…' He met the warmth in her eyes and, drawn like a magnet, came down beside her. 'I love you so much but I was shattered when you walked out four years ago. When Pandora called in at the office this afternoon and was really frank about how she had behaved then, I realised that I'd made a lot of mistakes too. I didn't give you enough support and I should've noticed the way she was behaving—'

'It's not important; it's all in the past, forgotten…'

Molly cut in unsteadily, tugging him down to her with his tie, only one motive in view as she angled her eager mouth up blissfully to the descending charge of his.

Passion surged up and concluded conversation for a long time after that. Not until they lay wrapped in each other's arms in a blissful haze of contentment did Molly recall something that had niggled at her earlier. 'Can't Pandora have children?'

'Her father's violence caused internal damage.' Sholto grimaced in disgust as he made the admission. 'She had an operation but the doctors really don't know if it's possible for her to have a child of her own.'

Molly rubbed her cheek ruefully against his shoulder. 'I'll never, ever be jealous of her again, Sholto. I just hope it all works out for her.'

A year later, Molly received a warm embrace from the woman she had come to regard as a sister-in-law. Pandora and Armando had flown over to Templebrooke to attend the important occasion of little Jasper Cristaldi's christening. Pandora's blue eyes had a deep inner glow of excitement and happiness.

'Guess what?' Pandora began when they were standing at the font.

The Reverend Donald Seaton gave her a gently reproving look as he baptised the baby in Molly's arms. Jasper set up a screech that would have wakened the dead and everybody burst out laughing. Molly's eyes met Pandora's and she understood and instantly she started to smile too.

Pandora was four months pregnant and wanted to shout it to the world but it was some time before the youngest and newest member of the Cristaldi family allowed her to share her feelings in any depth.

After a celebratory lunch, Molly and Sholto saw off

Donald and his wife, a friendly and attractive young woman he had met and fallen in love with while he was in New Zealand. Armando and Pandora departed next, hand in hand and like a pair of teenagers with a secret that made them smile a lot and rather reluctant to spend too much time around other people. Nigel and Lena herded together their children. They were never very comfortable at Templebrooke, no matter how hard Sholto worked at making them relax, and usually departed as soon as they decently could.

'So you don't think he'd mind...?' Nigel whispered urgently on the front steps. 'And you'll discuss it with him?'

'You should do it yourself,' Molly groaned, irritated that her brother was still so intimidated by her husband and cuddling Jasper close in consolation.

'What was all that about?' Sholto enquired darkly as he closed a possessive arm round his wife's rather tense shoulders and walked her back into the house. 'What wouldn't I mind?'

'Nigel doesn't feel he's really cut out for the business world. And he *has* been working for that company of yours for a whole year now...'

'He wants to take over the garden centre again, doesn't he?' Sholto closed his eyes in barely concealed horror at the prospect.

'He hasn't done very well on this training course idea, has he?'

Sholto angled an anxiously assessing eye at Molly's concerned face. 'He tries; he tries very, very hard.'

'He doesn't want the responsibility of running the garden centre again,' Molly said worriedly. 'He gets on well with that manager you put in and now that the centre has been expanded again he was wondering if he could

sort of…well, take over the horticultural end and leave
the rest to that manager…'

Sholto's tension evaporated and he burst out laughing.
'Molly…why do you think I expanded the place? It was
important that Nigel gained some understanding of how
a business should operate but I am more than happy for
him to concentrate his considerable knowledge where it
will be most profitably employed.'

In perfect harmony, they climbed the stairs. Sholto
laid Jasper down in his cot with exaggerated care, tucked
him in and smiled down into the drowsy dark eyes so
like his own. 'He's just perfect, isn't he?'

'You could not produce anything less than a perfect
child,' Molly teased, but she was touched as she always
was by the unashamed love and affection which Sholto
made no attempt to hide around their son.

'But then I have a perfect wife…' Sholto curved her
into his arms with a deep sigh of satisfaction.

Molly leant back into the embrace of his long, hard
body and with a slight flush on her cheeks registered his
masculine response to that proximity. She gave a sinuous
shiver and turned round in the circle of his arms, heart
beating as fast as it ever had as she looked up into loving
and amused dark golden eyes.

'Early night?'

'It's only five o'clock.'

Molly knew that look of mock disapproval, recognised the pleasure in his gaze as she propositioned him.
'I want you *now*…'

Sholto claimed her mouth in an electrifying kiss and
backed her out of the room, across the landing and into
their bedroom.

'I'll never stop wanting you, *cara*…' And with blissful contentment Molly melted into his arms.

**Make a Valentine's date
for the premiere of**

⬧ HARLEQUIN® **Movies**

starting February 14, 1998 with

Debbie Macomber's

This Matter of

Marriage

on the movie channel tmc

Just tune in to **The Movie Channel** the **second Saturday night** of every month at 9:00 p.m. EST to join us, and be swept away by the sheer thrill of romance brought to life. Watch for details of upcoming movies—in books, in your television viewing guide and in stores.

If you are not currently a subscriber to The Movie Channel, simply call your local cable or satellite provider for more details. Call today, and don't miss out on the romance!

*100% pure movies.
100% pure fun.*

Makes any time special.™

shocking pink

THEY WERE ONLY WATCHING...

The mysterious lovers the three girls spied on were engaged in
a deadly sexual game no one else was supposed to know about.
Especially not Andie and her friends whose curiosity had deep-
ened into a dangerous obsession....

Now fifteen years later, Andie is being watched by someone who
won't let her forget the unsolved murder of "Mrs. X" or the
sudden disappearance of "Mr. X." And Andie doesn't know who
her friends are....

WHAT THEY SAW WAS MURDER.

ERICA SPINDLER

Available in February 1998 at your favorite retail outlet.

**The Brightest Stars
in Women's Fiction.™**

MIRA

HARLEQUIN ◆ PRESENTS®

REVENGE
is Sweet
—when it leads to love!

Look out for this irresistible new trilogy
by popular Presents author
Sharon Kendrick:

March 1998:
GETTING EVEN (#1945)

April 1998:
KISS AND TELL (#1951)

May 1998:
SETTLING THE SCORE (#1957)

Three lavish houses, three glamorous couples—
three passionate reasons for revenge....

Available wherever Harlequin books are sold.

Don't miss these Harlequin favorites by some of our top-selling authors!

HT#25733	THE GETAWAY BRIDE	$3.50 U.S. ☐	
	by Gina Wilkins	$3.99 CAN. ☐	
HP#11849	A KISS TO REMEMBER	$3.50 U.S. ☐	
	by Miranda Lee	$3.99 CAN. ☐	
HR#03431	BRINGING UP BABIES	$3.25 U.S. ☐	
	by Emma Goldrick	$3.75 CAN. ☐	
HS#70723	SIDE EFFECTS	$3.99 U.S. ☐	
	by Bobby Hutchinson	$4.50 CAN. ☐	
HI#22377	CISCO'S WOMAN	$3.75 U.S. ☐	
	by Aimée Thurlo	$4.25 CAN. ☐	
HAR#16666	ELISE & THE HOTSHOT LAWYER	$3.75 U.S. ☐	
	by Emily Dalton	$4.25 CAN. ☐	
HH#28949	RAVEN'S VOW	$4.99 U.S. ☐	
	by Gayle Wilson	$5.99 CAN. ☐	

(limited quantities available on certain titles)

AMOUNT	$ _____
POSTAGE & HANDLING	$ _____
($1.00 for one book, 50¢ for each additional)	
APPLICABLE TAXES*	$ _____
TOTAL PAYABLE	$ _____

(check or money order—please do not send cash)

To order, complete this form and send it, along with a check or money order for the total above, payable to Harlequin Books, to: **In the U.S.:** 3010 Walden Avenue, P.O. Box 9047, Buffalo, NY 14269-9047; **In Canada:** P.O. Box 613, Fort Erie, Ontario, L2A 5X3.

Name: _____

Address: _____ City: _____

State/Prov.: _____ Zip/Postal Code: _____

Account Number (if applicable): _____

*New York residents remit applicable sales taxes.
Canadian residents remit applicable GST and provincial taxes.

Look us up on-line at: http://www.romance.net

075-CSAS